Praise for *Under the Influence*

"J.C. Ellefson's *Under the Influence: Shoutin' Out to Walt* pulls Whitman back to the center stage, and electrifyingly reminds us that *Writing is Mystical Revelation Or Nothing At All*. Ellefson, thank God, is lovingly wild wide-eyed in hard-fought ways, and golly, do we need him now. This book simply made me more alive."

—Tom Paine, Author of *Scar Vegas* and *The Pearl of Kuwait*

For Rowshan,
Thank you so much
for your big lit smile
and in-person
spot light.

UNDER THE INFLUENCE:
Shoutin' Out to Walt

All Best.

Jim

J.C. Ellefson
Summer's Gale Farm

Fomite
Burlington, VT

ISBN-13: 978-1-944388-07-2

Library of Congress Control Number: 2017948837

Fomite

58 Peru Street

Burlington, VT 05401

www.fomitepress.com

Acknowledgements

Antigonish Review: "Save that Tiger"; "Reconstructing the Entire Institution at Brown's Stables"

Atlanta Review: "Walt Whitman Shows Up for Dinner"

Beacon Street Review: "An Epistolary Re-Connection with the Old Man"

Centennial Review: "Getting Into the University of the Road"

Borderlands: The Texas Review: "The Way It Works"

Boston Phoenix: "What's Happening Today..."

Centennial Review: "A Cerebral Return to the Grave of Hattie..."

Gulf Stream: "What to Say..."

Hampden-Sydney Poetry Review: "Back on the Ghost Road"; "What It Looks Like and How to Mean It"

Literary Review: "Jumping Jim's Poetry Emergency"

Madison Review: "Deacon Bill's Sermon Concerning Work"

National Forum: "Walt Whitman Bids Adieu to the Graduating Class..."

New Orleans Review: "Riding Lesson"

New York Quarterly: "Lloyd Waxes Hypothetical on the Ramparts of New Jersey"

Nimrod: "How Nalungiac Befriended the Wolves"

Orbis: "Letter of Thanks to the Incomparable Doctor Brother..."

Paris/Atlantic: "The August Birthdays at Family Camp"

Permafrost: "...Nature Boy"

Pilgrimage: "The Entire Ninth Grade Contra Dances..."

Plaza: "Walt Whitman's Letter of Thanks after Skating All Day..."

Rattle: "Looking for an Angel—Friday Night"; "Last Words of Encouragement..."

Santa Barbara Review: "In Dreams a Boy Heads West..."

This book is for my soul brother, William J. Everts Jr. Known as Wild Bill to some, and The Wildman to many; Bill is the only guy who can hum a Billie Holiday tune—while nailing your feet to the floor during a discussion about why Shakespeare had to kill off Mercutio—while consuming fresh ice-caught Lake Champlain perch, generously and eloquently served with the starting rotation of the Philadelphia Phillies, frim fram sauce, with shafafa on the side.

Wild Bill, know that as long as I can do it, I'll remain howling in your direction.

"Not a single moment, old beautiful Walt Whitman,
have I stopped seeing your beard full of butterflies..."
Federico Garcia Lorca

"Walt Whitman is in everything."
Unknown — Shouted over the din in a packed dining hall at the Breadloaf Campus, Ripton, Vermont. The voice belonged to a young woman.

CONTENTS

Walt Whitman Shows Up For Dinner

He knew how to hoot at the front door, and how
to wander around back when there was no response.

And he knew how to zero-in on our
big, green Canadian rocker, and how to
linger, smile at something off in the distance
totally without discomfort until the extra plate
appeared, heaped with noodles, salad on the side
all riding on his lap, his huge eyes getting shiny
—then going underwater

                          and for that moment
we could see everything he saw: we could see
blood of dying boys in a military hospital; we could
see rafts of round silky women holding Asian
parasols in the middle of Brooklyn Bridge.

It was like that—while he stayed for nearly an hour
he used extra salt, ate everything in small
bites, the dogs and kids twice knocked off his
magnificent straw hat, everybody
hollering: Please. Everybody hollering: Mercy.
Everybody hollering: Astronomy

                            —that is, until
he laughed. Yes indeed, had a laugh on him, that one.

He left grinning, high stepping his long
vertically connected bones for the Gap Road, the place
in the mountains where we see the moon rise, so I

thought I'd track the old boy, but the prints
stopped looking human.

Now there's no sleeping—feel like my heart's
in my ears, the whole world talking outside my
window, and sure I love every black and white
cow, and sure, I love golden retriever
dogs, every brown trout, every song
the shoulder high grass sings
to itself is the song I sing. I sing
love out loud to the cows.

                           OK, keep
your cows, Give me a mob. Give me a mob
on Brooklyn Bridge.

                   OK, forget the bridge.
Give me a gun metal grey B.M.W. going
90 the wrong way down a slick one way
street in the middle of the night

                        —Oh, I love
every dark and fair-haired boy and girl, every
grand dad and granny dancing so close you can't
slip a piece of paper between
cheek and cheek is the way I feel. I
feel

      stop it. Stop it. I love George W.
Bush. I love Saddam Hussein. Oh
hell, I love everybody, everybody, everybody.

WHAT TO SAY WHEN YOUR FOUR-YEAR-OLD RAPSCALLION NIECE ASKS: ARE YOU GOING TO LEAVE ME WHEN YOU DIE?

"All goes onward and outward, nothing collapses,
And to die is different from what anyone supposed, and luckier."
Walt Whitman

I'll be the thirty-nine geese flying over
Grandfather's broken wooden house a little
out of season—when you were just
thinking of geese—flying so low you can
feel the wing breeze on your face. Or I'll be
the morning low lying fog—sticking together
all the envelopes, all the stamps before
the letters get mailed. Or the church bell
when it rings abrasively off time, or the lunch
invitation delivered by the amazingly
handsome young man who goes
on to say: Anything you order is all
right with him. Anything you want. I'll be
the round words in his mouth, or perhaps
the idea. I'll be the idea that makes your car
roll for miles when it's out of gas, or I'll be
the idea that shrinks the strange, China red
slipper three sizes to fit your foot. You see—

it's just the way it works. The years will put
unfathomable dark water between us, and well—
you won't be able to see me waving to you so
far away, free and wild—but I'll be the idea
that puts a silver ring around the moon

—perfect and beautiful—so perfect and beautiful
you'll wake up somewhere in the deep
night in Grandfather's broken wooden house, look
out the dusty, fly speckled western window
and smile almost inside out—for the

beauty of it—this moon and this world
I mean—the world between the inspired
fashionable young woman in the window
dressed in the star-spangled yellow
robe and purple tights, and the idea
shaking all the leaves in the trees into refined
whisper. I'll be whispering: Listen. I'll be
whispering: It's all right. It's all right.

IN DREAMS A BOY HEADS WEST ALONG THE GHOST ROAD

"We were together. I forget the rest."

Walt Whitman

You are behaving yourself, walking down
some feathery plum-lined street—a little
glide in your stride, well-pressed, hair parted
distinctively to the side of your head—on a day
so quiet and serene you could be inside
a Monet. You are there. You are there and maybe
half a foot of flower blossoms fill up
the avenue. Oh, yeah. It's
incredible. The blossoms are so deep you don't
hear the tires rolling up behind you. You
don't even hear the window rolling down. You only
hear the shout. This is
how it happens. They are

there: the old man, the dog, even the green
Pontiac coup. And they've been
looking for you for over thirty years through
miles of plowed fields, blue highways, mosquito-ridden
junk yards. They've spent over thirty years
wandering through every preferred and non-preferred
residential small-town community at dinner time
looking for your distinctively picturesque Norman
Rockwell face at a wooden table—eating
fried chicken, corn on the cob, strawberry-
rhubarb pie—and now, they are

here, all right: the man who should have been

your father, the neurotic dog who was your best
friend, even the intrepid Pontiac coup that bore
the three of you to infinite locations of unsurpassed
fun and high adventure. And somehow they never
gave up. When you threw up your hands and went
south, they went south. When you traveled through
Asia, so did they. Hell, they've been looking for you
everywhere, and incidentally, they're looking
pretty good—the man in his red shirt, jaunty
straw hat, after-shave; the dog quivering
at attention and all brushed out. They're looking
so good you'd never know they were dead. No
one would ever know. And when the old man

asks you to hop in, you don't
hesitate. You turn into their twelve year old
pal, filthy shorts and shirt, and hop
in, shaking hands like you mean it with the old
man, putting your arm around the crazy high-
strung setter dog. And then you smile. In fact, if
someone were to look inside the car, that's what
they'd see: one huge smile careening
west into the afternoon sun, traveling at twice
the speed of time, until every cool-running
car has big fins, the gas is cheap, and trees
canopy the road where fortune, distance and defeat
are unknown abstract concepts along a highway
famous for keeping its mouth shut. Like
you. Like the old man who flips down his

sun-glasses, and then grips the lime-green
wheel of the Pontiac at ten and two, or like
the dog who sighs and puts his head on his master's
shoulder, and then yours. And you are

there, and you're not
talking—the boy with the wind on his
face, grinning into the wild western sun like he's
just gotten away with something—one hell of one
god-damn grin. Grinning like there's no tomorrow.

WHAT'S HAPPENING TODAY—HERE AND IN THE GREAT BEYOND
(For My Mother—1926-1972)

"And what I assume you shall assume,
For every atom belonging to me as good belongs to you."

Walt Whitman

I live alone in a tumble-down log house six
miles off the fringe from a spandex, cappuccino
town—well out of the prevailing wind blow—three
deer in the yard, bobcat, Fearless Ross—the fighting
weasel, twelve foot heroically hand dug
spring well, twelve foot heroically hand dug
big ideas coming out of ground so hard
you'd think you're in a concrete high rise urban
cul-de-sac, which you're not, by the way, which

you're not. Strongest coffee in the capital free
world, house coyote, communist green tea, two
china cups, full moon, gibbous moon, moon
holding water, extensive and far reaching
library, yellow gas lights, five forks, optimism
knowing no quarter—fearless optimism. Why, just

look at me. I am writing to you as if you can
read. I am writing to you as if you can
see inside everything I've become, as if it means
something to you, as if you'll read what I
write, throw your head back and laugh
all afternoon. You. Now. Watch me light all these
candles. See? Are you laughing? Happy Birthday.

WAKE

It may have been about emotional
rescue or redemption

                        —or it may have been about
the weather
                horizontal rain blowing
the hair right off your head, and then freak
snow against the orange leaves.

                                Or the focus
could have been about how wine creates
community amongst previously feuding
relatives, who were nothing
short of hysterical:
                        my Louisiana
grandfather saying everything was as dark
as the inside of a horse; my good Aunt Marie
ripping out a laugh about her sister, and then
shrieking her way for the bathroom; or my
grandma's anaconda hug. Good God
the woman could maneuver her shoulder
right into your Adam's Apple and start
some serious, constricting loving—the room
spinning around dolphin-esque

voices repeating "Vive la mort," "Lamb
of God," "Home to Jesus,"

and I'm thinking, Yeah
Jesus, things are bad enough without blowing
lunch on the Old Man's sacred
Scandinavian goat rug

—the intrepid Old
Man—who pulled a characteristic
Houdini: when someone mentioned
reinforcement beverages, he grabbed
his wallet and disappeared, and when he
rematerialized the next morning, the sorry
bastard still wasn't there.

But then Claire
shows up on Buddy, riding the seven
miles in the full gale, forgot her
gloves, she says, tying him up
to the porch railing, Buddy
putting his rump to the weather and Claire
so cold she can barely talk

but that's
what we do in the kitchen, a shot
of Jameson's apiece, Claire burying
her face in my shirt, leaving an impressive
wet spot the size of a pie plate. "I'm
so sorry," she says. I agree, and laugh. We
laugh, not because we're misanthropic
sociopaths, but because we love
a good, absurd double
entendre.
Fifteen minutes later she's back up

wearing my black Korean War issue
surplus gloves with the green wool liners.

      "Those are for good," I say, and I look at her
like I know what that was about, too, but I
didn't know.

                I didn't know anything.

                              I didn't

even know about the miracle of memory: how you
can wake an hour before dawn on some steamy
mid-summer morning and be nineteen and fifty
at the same time. I didn't know how the dead
can lean back, crack a big sudsy beer smile
and speak, or how a fifteen year old girl
can get a hold on you.

                 Yes, indeed
a fifteen-year-old horse girl can lay her
rough, quiet hands on your shoulders, bury her
face in your holey wool shirt—and then ride home

—you, her, and her bone pile pony forever
disappearing into a series of freezing white hills.

WHAT IT LOOKS LIKE AND HOW TO MEAN IT

"There are who teach only the sweet lessons of peace and safety;
But I teach lessons of war and death to those I love,
That they readily meet invasions, when they come."

Walt Whitman

A man takes a shotgun and blows a hole at your feet—
telling you to never forget what it looks like, never
forget what it can do. You easily agree while
looking at a smoldering hole wider than
a coffee can. The man smiles, there's a soft
breeze, a black and white setter dog comes over and leans
against your legs, the grass is brown amongst
scotch pine, and the man tells you with a certain
amount of sternness and delight, if you ever
do this to somebody, you better mean it.

It really happens like this. You are twelve—
gangly, clumsy, and of otherwise no
redemption. The man is your neighbor—red
hair, big sad droopy eyes, and he loves
to teach you; he loves you so much he should
have been your father, and you often
pray for a switch. You pray, but what you get is
how to put a sweet twenty gauge to your shoulder and become
a diamond, and years later when the man's wife tells her
sad story of the gun going off, smoke, thump on the floor

you get to go back to his pine grove and watch jeweled
crows circle out of range, while you concentrate on her

face, her eyes, her mouth, watching her cry and laugh
at the same time. A woman with such an exquisite
sense of absurdity she tells you, he might have died
with a smile on his face, but there wasn't
a smile—there wasn't even a face, and when she cries
her words cover you, and when she cries, you see
a smoldering hole in the ground, and it's

amazing for you—how it happens—and it
continues to amaze you during the drive back up
north when you see the same droopy eyes in a dozen
sad faces in a dozen non-descript passing
cars. Amazing—how this world works. One moment you're
prodigiously and unredeemingly twelve, the next
you're watching an old woman cry and laugh, and the next

you're driving along a long divided highway, repeatedly
passing a red-haired dead man and his wagging-tailed
setter dog, because it really is like this, you really
do hold the wheel tight in your clumsy, gangly hands.
You even, as the afternoon wears on, manage to wave
back at them because it's like that too, or because
there's an utter lack of authority and precedent—
or because you're lucky enough to remember exactly
what it looks like—and how to mean it.

UPON THE CUSP OF SUMMER, WALT WHITMAN AND A BRIGHT COMPANION CONVERGE ON THE BRISTOL VILLAGE CREEMEE STAND

Years from now this day will be reduced
into nothing—inconsequence—another
blissfully hot late afternoon where the light
drops down into evening

                      —but today

the little girl is wearing a magic
ring of what is certainly real
gold. Today she is riding her fat tire
bike for the first time sans
training wheels

                 —jubilant, immaculately
focused on the sidewalk ahead, heading
for ice cream. She is five and fearless.

The man is forty-five and awkwardly racing
headlong beside her, bent back, knees—his
hands floating over the handlebars.

                               He is

focused on hurling his body earthward to soften
a possible fall. He is focused on pitching himself
against his own imagined tide of rural on-coming
muscle cars, logging trucks, the local
pack of snarling Harleys. He will lay them all
asunder, and if necessary, scatter their metallic
oil-blackened bits to the four winds

                         —and as his

heroic resolve rises to red-faced
fury, she turns to him and says, Let go.

But this is impossible. The man can't let go. He can
only see the road ahead laying for her. He can
only hear her wails and cries, the gravel
scooping out the soft butter skin of her
knees—her palms in ribbons
of hamburger, traumatic head wounds, months
of reconstructive facial surgery, the extended
family falling apart outside the emergency
room, watching the revolutions of a clock
with no hands.
                He can even see entire
confederations of hell-bred Rottweilers
appearing out of the gutters to snap
the sneakers right off her pedals.

                                        And as he

looks ahead, he knows the road
is wily, covetous of everyone's small
burning heart, everyone's
smooth perfect skin.

                          She looks ahead and sees
the special flavor of the day—chocolate
dipped; rainbow sprinkled; sugar coned; with mixed
nuts; hot, red cinnamon hearts; honey
caramel; cherry on top.
                          She looks ahead and sees
all her friends, their parents, aunts, and uncles
queuing up at the counter, her favorite baby-sitter

taking her order, the speed and good
humor with which it arrives, and the race
to eat it all before it sublimates
into gravel and grass.

                      With this in mind
she turns to him and says: I can do it. It's
OK if you let me go.

                    And he lets her
go, but it's some strange alien
force that loosens the man's
grip on the handlebars and allows her
to drift away from him, crack
by crack over the sidewalk, as he
races stiff legged, stiff backed
behind her, the faint murmur of front
porch well-wishers in his ears, along
a maple-lined street that could go on
forever, or go on until
all interested parties miraculously arrive
unscathed at the village creemee stand.

Getting Into The University Of The Road

(Take Walt's Advice)

The Dean's the high-miles bicycle man with the dark
splotches on his wings—and a grin that has
roamed the American west from water hole
to water hole in search of some job that doesn't
shorten his leash between dinner and breakfast.
Or the Dean's the blissful hog-eyed woman
on the bus with the tan-bark face, carrying her
life in the paper sack on her lap, or the little
girl playing in the sage brush with her yellow
world dog, three stars, rising moon and a deep
blue sky. You have to ask them if they'll

teach you. You have to ask them if you can
wake up in the freezing night in the middle
of the desert and listen to wheel music
rise and fall along the loneliest
highway in America—or ask them
why the waitress in Nowhere, Nevada calls
everybody "Honey," and why it
jingles the change in your pockets, and puts
another hum into your wheels along
hundreds of miles of pitifully oblivious
dark road. Or just get personal. Ask them

if the road signs lie, or if you will ever
arrive wherever it is you're going, or if
the going will always be good—praise

God, the Mother, and all the roaming angels.
Be sure to get personal and praise all
the roaming angels—as if this time they'll let you
in, this time you'll get there—roll right
through a wide door into a frenzy of black
gowns, tubas, violins, mortar board hats, everybody
shouting, "Oh Yeah!" Praise them so you can
become the sweet solemn-eyed old man, trembling
fingers on the steering wheel in the greatest
of anticipations—the sweet solemn-eyed
old man whose face fractures into a grin
whenever anyone says, "It's time to go."

Leaves Of Grass

At close to thirty, Oliver's champion Percheron stud, Chief Joseph, was mostly blind, but he still knew when there was a mare in the barn. We watched Oliver lead him out of his stall with the lead line chain shank over his nose. The horse was quiet as a bale of hay, but when he gave the slightest hesitation, Oliver would jerk down hard on that chain and hit him across the neck and muzzle with a miniature baseball bat. Already Oliver's face was close to blood red; veins popped out on his forehead, and he was spitting words none of us could understand. The barn filled with chain rattle, the pounding of feet—and the dull thuds of the bat.

From across the floor, I could see Jack wince, close his eyes and shake his head. Then the stud started to dance, leap to his hind feet, once pulling Oliver clear off his. When they got close to the mare, Joe threw his head in the air, knocking the club out of the old man's hand. The mare stomped, screamed back, and kicked wildly behind her. The stud arched his neck, sprang again to his hind end, whirled towards the mare, pawing the air in front of him so fast his legs disappeared. He caught Oliver once hard on the shoulder, then grazed him on the side of his head. The stud crashed down, squealed, and then bounced back up. The old man stood below, foaming at the mouth, shouting. I saw him grit his teeth, lower his head, and jerk down for everything he was worth on the lead line. Then there was another kind of scream, and everybody in that barn heard Oliver's arm crack like a piece of splintering wood.

Oliver sank to the floor without another word. Jack jumped out and took over, and as soon as he did, the stud was a different horse. In a few minutes, it was all over, and Joe lumbered back to his stall.

The mare's owner was this guy with quite a bit of mousse in his hair—and a furry felt white Stetson. He had driven eight hours from outside of Toronto to breed his Percheron mare, but he might as well have arrived from Mars.

"Wham, bam, thank you ma'am," he kept saying. "Wham, bam, thank you, ma'am. That stud's Mr. Wham, isn't he? Did you see that? Did you see that? Think that boy has some lead in his bullets? Should have taken some pictures of before and after. Wasn't thinking. I could have had this on my Facebook. Did you see that?"

He was looking straight at me, so I nodded. Jack was leaning over Oliver, who was quietly crying on the barn floor. Within minutes, we had him in the truck and on the way to the hospital. He was flushed-faced, ghostly, holding up his left arm with his right, and there was a large scrape on his right ear and cheek. By now, both he and Jack knew the route pretty well. Over the last ten years, everything had gone to hell, but it wasn't always like that.

In the beginning, even Oliver Branch's barn had pillars. The house looked like it was a southern plantation: wrap-around porch, portico, sun room, carriage entrance, double-etched glassed mahogany front doors, manicured boxwood hedges, swimming pool. You could start mowing the lawn on Monday, and not finish until Thursday. Like the main house, the stone eighteenth century tenant house was on the national registry, and at one time, Oliver ruled over one thousand acres. At the high water mark, he had seventeen champion Morgans and Percherons; four milk cows; a full-time hired man, woman, and family; perpetually smiling wife Shirley; a set of twins—track star Butch who looked just like him; and a daughter, Betty, who looked exactly like her mother, except Betty never smiled. She was the state champion in a number of equine events. My favorite and definitely the most exciting was "Fastest Around the Ring," where she was the national champ. Professional riders came from all over and tried to beat her; nobody came even close.

"Wish we had a horse farm," I'd tell my mother with my hang-dog face.

"Well, we don't. We have a two-hundred-fifty-year-old sway-back house that's built out of field stone, horse hair, and lime mortar, and every morning when I wake up and make my way down to this sway-back kitchen, I look up and love every crack in the plaster ceiling."

My mother was doing that thing she did with her teeth. She'd set them hard, and her whole jaw was like an anvil. You could pound steel on it.

"I'm not saying that I don't love this house, Mom. I'm just saying that I'd love to work for Oliver and learn how to do everything. Be his hired man sometime, maybe. He knows how to do everything with a horse. If someone wanted a horse to jump over the moon, he could make it happen."

"Yes, I have no doubt that Oliver Branch could make a horse jump through the eye of a needle. Not sure about the how-he-does-it part, though," my mother said. "One time I saw him beat a horse until it bled, and then he beat it for bleeding. And sometime I'll tell you why those kids of his are so fast. They know how to get out of his way."

As an eleven-year-old, I did get a chance to work at the Branch's during haying. It was killer work but always a great time. The only downside was the barn. I'd get spooked in the catacombs of it all. It felt ghostly, like one huge box of shadows, like bad things had happened in there, and it all had seeped deep into the wood. But Oliver was fun enough. He'd grab a huge armful of hay, draw it up to his face, breathe it in and shout, "Lord have mercy. Can you feel the power of it?"

And he'd crack endless dumb jokes. "Are you working hard, Jimmy, or hardly working? I've told you a million times never to exaggerate. Do you know what fun spelled backwards is? It's nuf. Call me anything, but don't me late for dinner." And always, right in the middle of some breakdown disaster, when the hay elevator quit, or the front tire of the tractor went flat, thunder storm starting to flash in the distance threatening to ruin everything, he'd start reciting from *Leaves of Grass*. Knew it all in a James Earl Jones booming baritone theatrical voice.

> *"A child said, What is the grass?* fetching *it to me with full*
> > *hands;*
> *How could I answer the child?. . . .I do not know what it*
> > *is any more than he.*
> *I guess it must be the flag of my disposition, out of hopeful*
> > *green stuff woven.*
> *Or I guess it is the handkerchief of the Lord,*
> *A scented gift and remembrancer designedly dropped,*
> *Bearing the owner's name someway in the corners, that we*
> > *may see and remark, and say Whose?*
> *Or I guess the grass is itself a child. . . .the produced babe*
> > *of the vegetation."*

After six hours of breathing chaff, getting tarred and feathered with the stuff in the mow, I'd ride my bike home and proudly show my mother my sweat-smeared five dollar check. She'd almost smile, do that snort thing she did sometimes, and say, "Just don't spend it all in one place."

Shirley Branch was endlessly smiling, and between hay loads, she'd make us come down for drinks and carrot cake. She made the best apple mint tea. After a couple of glasses, my eleven-year-old self felt like it could hold up the entire barn and throw it into the mow with my chicken wing arms, and you could go to Alaska for five years and live off that carrot cake. Shirley was also the strongest woman I knew. She was six feet tall, could throw a bale as far as any man, and her long, dark brown braid would twirl around her head. She got right into it, too, with the animals. One time, in the summer, I saw the bruises on her arms and shoulders. When I asked her about it, she said, "When you live on a farm, Jimmy, you get beat up. Take care of horses and cows. Things happen."

Shirley was my mother's best friend, and sometimes, late at night, long after I had gone to bed, Shirley would show up, and they'd drink coffee and talk clear to dawn. My father had been dead for a couple of years by then, and there was no umpire in the house, nobody telling anybody anything, no dark cloud, no Darth Vader. A few times, I'd hear them from my bedroom. They'd get a little loud, high-pitched, and I couldn't tell if they were laughing or crying. To me, as a kid, it all sounded the same. Sometimes Shirley was there in the morning when I got up, and so happy to see me, saying how quiet her house was now that Butch and Betty were at Penn State. The three of us would eat breakfast as the sun came up, and both of them would be there in the window, waving as I boarded the bus to school.

One February morning, though, was a little different. My mother woke me up at 4:30 and told me to get dressed. I had to come down and help. Shirley was in the kitchen. She was elevating her leg on a chair. She had a split lip and a bruise around her right eye. She tried to smile when she saw me.

"Jimmy, this morning Lulu's mad at the world. She just had a fit when I tried to milk her and caught me good with her back feet. Gave me a good one with her head."

My mother held me firmly by the shoulders and turned me around, her face in my face.

"I want you to go down to the Branch's and milk that cow. Their hired man has gone. You know how to do it, and you know how to do a good job. If that cow doesn't get milked, she's going to get sick."

"Yes, ma'am," I said.

I saw my mother set her teeth. She turned towards Shirley.

"Is he going to be OK?"

Shirley put a hand to her face and nodded her head.

"He's not family, Joanne. That's the difference."

My mother opened her eyes a little wider. Shirley waved me over, closer to her.

"Jimmy, make sure when you go in the milking parlor, tell Oliver who you are. Say, 'Good Morning, Mr. Branch. I'm here to help.' Be sure to say it nice and loud. He's a little deaf. Nice and loud. Lulu's at her stanchion waiting for you. I'm so sorry to ask. It's because Lulu is my cow, and when Oliver gets like this, he won't touch her."

The quarter mile walk down to the Branch's was beautiful in the deep cold. It was also a little frightening. Trees were cracking, the footing was icy, and nobody was on the road except me and the barred owls.

The Branch's milk parlor was all lit up, and when I walked in, instead of hay, milk, and manure, the place smelled sweet. I didn't see anyone at first, but I did what I was told.

"Good morning, Mr. Branch," I said real loud. "It's Jim Ellefson, and I'm here to help."

Then I spotted him. Oliver was sitting on a little milk stool in the corner, looking out the window at the dark. There was a gallon bottle at his feet. He wheeled around and locked his eyes on me, stood up, like something had scared him. His face was red, and he had been crying, snot all over his lips and mouth. I watched him roll his hands into fists, heard him snarl. The man had eyes like two fried eggs.

He started coming at me.

I said it again, and this time, I let it loose so Shirley and my mother could have heard me a quarter mile away.

"Mr. Branch, it's Jimmy. I'm here to help."

His face went slack, and he stood there nailed to the floor with his mouth open, teetering a little. Finally he nodded, and then almost smiled, turned and walked over to the Brown Swiss, who must have been the hardest cow in the world to milk.

Soon I could hear the milk shoot into his pail like someone had turned on a spurting hose. I walked over to Lulu who was quietly chewing her cud. She glanced at me for a couple of seconds and then went back to eating. Shirley's stool was turned over, and her pail was upside down on the damp bedding. I grabbed it, walked over to the sink and scrubbed it out well with soap and hot water.

"Milk should always be white," Shirley taught me, "and there are plenty of ways to keep it like that."

It must have taken me twenty-five minutes to milk that cow, even though Lulu stood like a statue the entire time. If she wasn't the nicest cow in the world, she was the second nicest, and there was no mystery about it. She was Shirley's. At eleven, I just wasn't very good at milking. I had just learned, but Oliver had milked three cows during the same time, moved the milk cans to the cooler, shoveled, swept out the bedding, and then moved on to feed the horses. When he left the milk parlor, the place was truly spotless, immaculate. Everybody around had jokes about it, along the lines of the three second rule. If you drop a cookie on a clean kitchen floor and pick it up within three seconds, that cookie is still good. If you drop a cookie on Oliver Branch's milk parlor floor, it's good after the entire day.

I could hear him talk to himself in the horse barn, and as he moved from stall to stall, his big James Earl Jones baritone voice started to boom.

"Prodigal, you have given me love—therefore I to you give love!
O unspeakable passionate love."

There was a short laugh, and then some banging, like he was hitting something with his fist.

"Do I contradict myself?
Very well then I contradict myself,
(I am large, I contain multitudes.)"

I wondered if the horses would stand up and applaud.

The light was coming up by the time I walked back to my own house for breakfast. I had blueberry pancakes with three eggs on top. Shirley said it was what Butch ate to make him so fast, so I did my best and almost finished. My mother was all smiles watching me pull on my green wool coat and hat. I knew I had done something good, something more than milking a cow, but I wasn't sure what it was. When she handed me my books on the way out the door, my hands ached. They would ache all day, and kids would rag me about smelling like a barn.

Shirley died when I was in seventh grade. My mother grieved for months afterwards, staring out the window at the dawn, drinking coffee, tears in her eyes.

"Heart failure," she said nodding hard. "Shirley Branch died of heart failure. Simple as that." And then her face would turn hard, and she'd pin me to the floor with a stare.

"What kind of man are you going to be, Jimmy Ellefson? Are you going to walk down the road followed by smiling dogs and kids and lame laying hens? Are you going to be the kind of man who sits down at someone's kitchen table and little children will run over and try to crawl into your lap? Or are you going to be the other thing?"

That stare of hers could burn a hole clear through boiler plate steel, but it wouldn't last long as soon as I spoke up.

"Mom, I'll always go for the smiling dogs and laying hens. You know that."

After Shirley's funeral, there were over three-hundred people at the Branch place. My mother spent the entire time with her arms around Butch and Betty. They stayed right by her side, too, and if their arms weren't around each other, they were holding hands.

"I'm your mother now," I heard her tell them, "and you have to do everything I say." Hard face.

Both of them started to laugh.

"You have to return to the sway-back house at every holiday. You have to stay with us at Christmas, and after a while, you have to build a house next door. I want your children crawling all over my kitchen."

Butch's smile faded when she got to the part about living next door. Betty looked at the floor.

For years until she died, Butch and Betty would send Mother's Day cards, Valentine's Day cards. My mother would send them both Christmas presents and checks on their birthdays. She went to their undergraduate and graduate commencements. When each of them got married, they flew my mother across the country to be with them, included her in the wedding party, highlighted her in the wedding pictures, always introduced her as "our mother," which was pretty funny considering both Butch and Betty were raven dark haired and big boned, and my mother looked like the girl who rode the polar bear in *East of the Sun and West of the Moon*. And when they started having kids, every single baby girl's middle name was Joanne.

Halfway through the wake, I watched them roar out of the dooryard in the hunter green three-quarter ton Chevy four by four Butch had built from scratch, and I had helped him. I had held the drop light. I stood there waving until the truck disappeared into the point at the end of the road. Both of their arms were out the truck windows waving back at me. I wouldn't see either of them for another fifteen years, but we certainly saw our share of Oliver Branch from a distance.

In a year, he had permanently lost his license, couldn't find a hired man to stay longer than a month, and soon started selling horses and land. By the time I was a high school senior, there was high brush growing between the house and barn, fields gone to milkweed and thistle. When I came back home after college, my high school friend Jack Marshall had bought Oliver's tenant house and ten acres—wanting to start a horse farm of his own. He could rent the barn—and maybe buy it later. Maybe more land, if there was any left.

"It was a hell of a deal," Jack told me. "And most of the time, Oliver's great. The house and barn are great, except for all the bottles. Everywhere. Took six truckloads out of this house to the dump. Took a month to make the place livable. Seriously. Broken windows, punched-in walls. Dead birds in the chimney. I mean, still, around here, when you pick up a stone, expect to find an Ernest and Julio Gallo wine bottle underneath it."

It was Jack who told me about Oliver's tack room. "It's right out of Miss Havisham and *Great Expectations*, Jim. Can't walk in there. The only thing missing is the wedding cake. Cobwebs from floor to ceiling covering priceless saddles, bridles, driving harnesses. Three-hundred blue ribbons if there's one, silver trophies, huge blown up pictures of all of them, one at the Eastern States Exhibition when Betty won the 'Fastest Around the Ring' national championship, Shirley's arm around Oliver, and Oliver standing up straight with his barrel chest, fierce bald head, glowing eyes and handlebar mustache. Hey, you want to get spooked, I'll show you. Like walking into a grave, man, and he won't let anybody close to it."

When Jack and Oliver got back from the hospital, we were all playing music in Jack's front parlor. Oliver had a cast from his shoulder to his wrist, and didn't seem to know anyone. When I asked him how he was, Jack did all the talking.

"This man broke his arm in two places and dislocated his shoulder."

There was a general gasp in the room, and I saw Jack's wife, Dorothy, look at him and shake her head. Jack nodded his big red head to her in affirmation, and then tried to smile.

"The doctor said the only good thing about it was that Oliver definitely got it all over at once. Done as much damage as he could. Can't do no more. Hospital wanted to keep him, but this old bird refused. Said he had to do chores in the morning. Isn't that right?"

Jack looked at Oliver and laughed, but Oliver just stood there.

After considerable encouragement, Dorothy did get him to sit down at the table and eat a big bowl of vegetable soup, but he managed to dribble most of it on himself before Dorothy put it in a mug instead.

"This will work better, Oliver," she said.

He looked up at her and spoke, but he was speaking about three or four inches to the left of her face.

"Thank you, Shirley," he said. The room got quiet for a moment.

We played for another hour and Dorothy sang "Fair and Tender Ladies," "Where the Nightingale Sings," and "John Riley." She was tall, had powerful arms, and her voice filled the room. Jack and Dorothy's little boy Rivendale insisted on sitting on my lap as I played fiddle, and somehow it worked. I told him that this was OK as long as he stayed three, but as soon as he was four, he'd have to sit in a chair of his own. There was very reluctant agreement. When someone asked about the next tune, Rivendale tapped me on the shoulder and pointed at his head.

"OK, everybody. We've just had a request for 'The Red-Haired Boy.'"

I kicked the tune off, and that little guy beamed. And of course we had to do our ritual at the end. I had to ask the magic question, as if I was looking for top-secret information.

"Now, who is the red-haired boy around here?"

"That's me, Uncle Jimmy." Rivendale giggled and buried his face in my shoulder.

It happened just about the time I was about to leave. There was a lull in the action, and Oliver started singing "My Bonnie Lies Over the Ocean" a cappella in a high tenor. Nobody could believe it was coming out of his mouth. Eerie, too. The man sounded like an angel.

Surely, this man has a halo somewhere, I thought. *Maybe he has little wings on his back.*

We all joined in on the chorus. "Bring back, oh bring back, oh bring back my Bonnie to me, to me."

Then Oliver sang a verse I had never heard.

"Last night as I lay on my pillow,

Last night as I lay on my bed,

Last night as I lay on my pillow,

I Dreamt that my Bonnie was dead."

It was nothing short of incantatory. I could see tears start to well-up in Dorothy's eyes, and Rivendale hugged me a little tighter. Everybody sang the chorus again, but Oliver wasn't finished.

"The winds have blown over the ocean,

The winds have blown over the sea,

The winds have blown over the ocean,

And brought back my Bonnie to me."

Nobody knew what to say afterwards. I started to wash some dishes since we had trashed the place. Rivendale marched off to bed with his copy of *All Creatures Great and Small*, giving me a long, significant look.

"Can he read that?" I asked Jack.

"Hell no, but you can. He wants to be a veterinarian."

"Might help with bills later," I said.

Jack was still chuckling when Oliver stood up and shuffled to the door without saying a word. Jack walked him out.

"Let me get you situated over there, Oliver."

Oliver waved him off with his good hand and kept walking.

"I'll be by in the morning to help out with chores. See you then."

The old man just kept on walking like he hadn't heard anything. Jack and I watched him make his way across the over-grown lawn and through the tangle of boxwoods. We heard his screen door bang, and then saw the yellow light go on in his kitchen.

It was mid-October, frost had already knocked out all the gardens, and fog was hovering waist-high over the fields. Full moon coming on Halloween night, and Rivendale talking incessantly about what he was going to be. A skunk. Dorothy was already making his black polyester fur suit, and Jack was going to rig up an invisible piece of fishing line to manipulate the tail.

"And when we go trick-or-treating, Uncle Jim, if I don't get candy, I will *wraise* my tail and spray." He gave what he called his scary laugh, and looked up at his father.

"Right, Dad?"

"That's right, buddy. They don't give you the candy, you give them the tail."

It frosted again hard that night. Ice on the windshields and water buckets. Hose frozen in the spigot. Frost was clinging to the split wood in the front yard and to the leaves of tall grass swaying in the fields. When Jack went over early the next morning to check on Oliver, he found him dead in the rocker by his cook stove. The cup of coffee was still warm in his hands.

A Good Man In An Emergency

"Stranger! if you, passing, meet me, and desire to speak to me,
why should you not speak to me?
And why should I not speak to you?"

Walt Whitman

Even in the driving snow, we could see that he
was a little blue bald man in a three piece
suit, shouting into a cell phone. After about five
minutes of watching him shout, the dog and I walked
down to where his big silver Ford one-ton had slid
into our driveway. Only one of the headlights
was working; the radiator was steaming; a fine grey
smoke was rising off the hood—out of the rusted
fenders; and from my angle, I could see some hot
red oil puddling-up under the transmission.

"Rusty thinks I have a bad plug," he said. "I'm
getting awful vibration."

Now, you have to understand, I am one
with the bright side of life. I wear bright yellow
happy-face T-shirts. I truly believe that there's an essential
miniature bluebird, at large, on the wing, in the very
center of my heart. When I see double rainbows, I start
trotting for the pot of gold. If I were imprisoned
in a room full of horse manure, I would immediately
dig for the pony.

But this man needed more that some
guy named Rusty. He needed more than Jesus. That's

right. Do not send the Son. A child wouldn't be able
to help this truck. No job for a boy, this guy
needed the Old Man, God, Himself. Hell, he needed
the entire Trinity, Mother Mary, plus the Pope.

"Bad plug," I said. "That ought to be easy to fix. Maybe
it's just a wire. Should we look?"

He nodded, I popped the hood, and the entire engine
burst into flames.
                                    An old woman with a creased
brown face appeared like she had just
come out of a bottle. Regardless, I pulled
the trigger on the fire extinguisher she handed me, and after
the initial over-shot, I smothered that engine with white foam.

Two cars whizzed by and threw slush on my dog, who had drifted
too close to the road. I yelled at him.

"Come on. We're having trouble enough without
you turning into a pancake."

He trotted over, and sat on my feet. I gave
the fire extinguisher back to the old woman, who stood there
shaking her head, smiling at the dog, and then at me.

"You remind me of my husband. He was a good man
in an emergency, too. Fix a car. Put out a fire. Two weeks
after we were married, our fishing boat sank. That man swam
three miles back to the beach with me digging my nails right into his
broad black shoulders—had a smile on his face the whole

time. That was him, all right. If he wasn't smiling, he
was just about to."

She paused, turned away and coughed, and then spit something
on the driveway that looked like the inside of a mouse.

"When my husband was alive, we had us a sweet dog, looked
just like *yourn*. She wouldn't let anyone near my baby. Growl. Carry
on. If you weren't family, she'd get in between
you and that crib, the hair standing
straight up on her back. Bit the doctor, my husband's
mother. Twice. That dog would have laid right
down in the mean gravely dust, fought, and died for my baby."

I told her she must have had herself quite a dog.

"Yeah, Boy. We called her Charity. Aunt Charity. Fourteen
years my little girl grew up with her. We lost Charity
the same year as my husband
                                                    wrapped her up
tight in my best red wool blanket and buried her
deep in the good dirt out back of my old house."

She reached down and stroked my boy's head, and then rubbed
behind his ears. Even in the cold wind, I could hear him
groan a little. He stretched out on the ice and rolled over.

"I had to sell that house three years ago. Nothing I could do."

The little blue man snapped his cell phone
shut and looked at us with a grin.

"Rusty says if we come right over, he'll replace that plug."

Little Blue ran around, jumped into the driver's seat—damn
if that beached leviathan didn't start, the greasy white foam
spitting all over the engine. I would have been far less
surprised if he had parted the Red Sea or made it rain
largemouth bass. I slammed the hood. She was climbing in
when she asked.

"What if we don't make it?"

"You guys just call me, right? Where you going?"

Both of them seemed to think that was the funniest thing they had
ever heard. She had her face in her hands. Tears streaming. Little blue
doubled over.

When Blue came up for air, I gave him my
number, and he punched it into his phone.

"Now, you keep your dog out of the road, young man."

I stood there and watched all the creases in her face
line-up in a smile, soft and bright, and then she started
coughing, but heavier this time. Shoulders
and head down, bent at the waist. A hard
cough. Under water, loamy dirt. And there was a fishing
boat, a little blue house, a garden out back with ten foot
silver corn, black dog asleep in the shade, a little girl holding
hands in the sun with a big, smiling black man with scratches
all over his wide shoulders.

                              Whatever it was inside her chest
wanted to make its way out.

She spit another mouse on the driveway, and then
came back to the surface. Eyes watering. Eyes closed.

"And you keep pancakes off the menu. You hear me?"

All of us started laughing again for some reason.

"Yes, Ma'am. Now, you call me if you don't make it."

"We'll make it," Little Blue piped up.

The old lady reached out and squeezed my hand
hard, and squeezed it again. "Now don't you
worry. I'll be waiting for you when you get there.
I know who you are."
                              Big brown eyes. Big brown smile.

I stood and waved both hands as Little Blue
roared off into the gale, fish-tailing
up into the point at the end of the road.

"You call me," I shouted after them, right out
loud, the snow biting my face. "Now, you call me, and I'll
come get you."

Neither of them waved back.
Neither of them turned around.

The Entire Ninth Grade Contra Dances
At Carol Waddington's Fourteenth Birthday Party

"I heard what was said of the universe,
Heard it and heard it of several thousand years;
It is middling well as far as it goes—but is that all?"

Walt Whitman

Anne Marshall wore a nineteenth century design peasant
dress that was bunched just inside her snowy
shoulders. Anne was my original partner for most
of the evening, and I kept thinking that dress didn't stand
much of a chance staying up if met with focused
resistance, but Anne's dress wouldn't be falling for some
guy into a pool of paisley rayon any time soon
—nor would anyone else's.

Somebody said the caller was Carol's
Uncle Jeff, and there was a family resemblance
considering his thin, lanky, gallinaceous frame. The man
had a huge grin, and whenever he stepped out to do
a demonstration, the top of his head reflected the immense
chandelier of the ballroom. Jeff had a pair of silver and black
cowboy boots, and wherever he went, he just floated. I want
to say "moonwalk" but Michael Jackson wouldn't moonwalk
for another fifteen years. Michael Jackson was still
a little kid. Michael Jackson was so young, he was still
black, and Martin Luther King would live for another
two months, unlike Carol's mother, who died of leukemia
two weeks before the party.

And then there was Carol, who
during the numerous punch breaks stood blank-faced

next to her father. I had seen that look before on kids when they didn't
make the baseball team, or were the ones left standing
in musical chairs. I remember Carol's father always
had his arm around her, but I can't remember
what she wore. In fact, I can't remember
ever talking to her in high school. By fourteen, she had figured out
how to disappear into the wallpaper, but tonight she was almost
famous, like she had just escaped from Red China, or won
the National Young Teens' Figure Skating Competition. No kid in that room
knew what she knew.

                            My mother told me on my way out, "You say
something nice to Carol Waddington tonight, and you let me know
what it was when you get home," but I never had much
of a chance to do it. Even during the numerous
punch breaks, Uncle Jeff would amuse us all with rope
tricks. The room's high ceiling was perfect, and that man
was one ball of fire, but he had to be: he was trying to sell
The Virginia Reel to a roomful of rockers, and we were ready
to diverge at every turn. Over ginger ale
Anne and her pals were mimicking Jimi Hendricks playing
guitar behind his back. Anne had just bought
Electric Ladyland and already knew most of the words. For my part, I had
curly blonde hair way over my collar

                                  Still, when the band started
jumping, the place exploded with stomping and howls, and yes, Jeff
traffic-controlled us through The Virginia Reel, The Texas
Star, Golden Stairs, and Lady of the Lake, but we
ended the evening with the traditional French Canadian
La Bastringue circle dance, where everyone passes off
a partner, and I did get a chance to dance with Carol—
who was a butterfly on her feet, having come from a contra dance

family, I guess. But when it came to swinging, that girl
was airborne. I had strong arms for a kid. I had been working
on hay crews, could throw an eighty pounder five feet
over my head, so I gave her a toss

                                           but Carol launched
herself, did that 360 without touching the floor, winged
or cabled, I don't know, up there past the chandelier and through
the roof into the clear starry blue-black mid-winter night sky
And I felt it too, that time when the world wants you more
than you want the world. I swear to you, she was on her
way. She could have visited inter-galactically, represented
Earth at The United Confederation of Astrophysical Beings—where mothers
never died, and flying antennaed mongrel dogs spoke
genial theoretical quantum mechanics. Everybody's
ears would be pointed, and they'd wear cool high collared
space clothes, no musical chairs, no wallpaper, no insolent
Jimi Hendricks impersonators

                             and Carol Waddington would have
made it if I didn't pull her back down. She would have left
that night, and all the ginger punch, Virginia Reels, and silver
boots in the world wouldn't bring her back.

                                   Carol was almost
smiling when she landed, that inside joke smile, that I've-
got-three-aces-and-two-kings-and-you've-got-nothing smile, smiling
like funny was a part of her original DNA code, and she could
wake with one of those half-way grins for the rest of her life without
ever revving up.

                              Carol was still almost smiling when we all
queued up to say so-long, thank you and good night, but by the time
it was my turn, Mrs. Marshall arrived to give her a hug that was a little
too long and a little too tight. I did get a chance to shake with Mr.

Waddington and Jeff, who reached out and squeezed
everybody Bob Dole style with his left hand because he was holding his coiled
trick rope in his right. "Thank you, Mr. Waddington, and I'm so
sorry," I said, and then watched his face go down under water
for a moment, and then come bobbing up. "Yes, thank you
James. It was great having you with us."

I walked out into cold
blue-black and got into my mother's cigarette infused
Country Squire station wagon, and she quizzed me for details on the entire
ride home, referred to Anne Marshall as my "little friend," and I made her
laugh about Jimi Hendricks and Uncle Jeff, and I told her I said
I was sorry, but not to Carol, and we both endured that silence
for a while.

But I didn't know anything about being sorry, but I
do now, and I want to tell you Carol Waddington, you
could leap, smiling girl, kick it higher than anyone I've ever seen, you
would have been a great inter-galactic representative for Earth, you
would have been able to put your arms around every green Aurora
Borealis blank-faced wallpaper girl, boy, or flying articulate
Andromeda dog standing outside of a circle in the entire
post Big Bang universe

and I'm sorry you never got to wear cool
high collared space clothes. I'm sorry I pulled you back from the blue-
black starry night ceiling and the immense crystal ballroom
chandelier, and, Carol Waddington, I am so sorry you lost your mother.

A Cerebral Return To The Grave of Hattie Mae Wilson Of The Defunct Alpha Alpha Missionary Baptist Church

"They pass—I also pass—anything passes—none can be interdicted…"
Walt Whitman

Hattie in the low ground. Hattie beside the falling
down church with the kicked apart piano, kicked apart
door. Hattie testifying beside the falling down
plaster, ceiling and roof, bees buzzing the yellow
roses growing in the foyer, or Hattie

bound for Glory with a quart mason jar of old Black-
eyed Susans plunked down by her tombstone, in the tall
grass, in the center of the disheveled
cemetery, in the shadow of the cold piss brick
church house wall. Jubilation, I guess. I
guess I'm supposed to shout jubilation—Lord
have mercy, say you got the Angel
Hattie in your band because she sure won't
pass this way again—hardly can read her
name on the limestone, next to the rags and smashed
whiskey bottles, the four and twenty blackbirds
singing in the eaves and I'm supposed to find
no fault in Him, and I find no fault in Him, but I
do for those sorry bastards and bitches who
defiled this House. Hattie, I know, I know I'm wide

awake five hundred miles away in the middle
of the night thinking I'll send you some FTD
Florist daisies in the morning—the ten

42

dollar bouquet—so this nice stammering white boy
dressed in a toga with silver wings on his bony
feet will arrive in a big puff of wind and fill
up your mason jar—or maybe I'll have him fill up
all the mason jars in every cemetery in the great
state of Pennsylvania, or maybe I could
re-roof, re-door, re-wire, re-window the church like
new, cut the grass, trim the yellow roses, sing

"Great Day Coming," in a brazen high voltage
devil-dog baritone to the accompaniment of four
and twenty blackbirds, or maybe my fingers will find
all the right notes on the brand new Baldwin—spare no
expense—piano. Lord be my witness. This is
what I'll do, Hattie Mae Wilson, may the Lord
have mercy on us all, little lamb, and may the Lord
be with you. May the Lord always be with you.

THE AUGUST BIRTHDAYS AT FAMILY CAMP

"This is the grass that grows wherever the land is
           and the water is,
This is the common air that bathes the globe.
This is the breath for America, because it is my
           breath,
This is for laws, songs, behaviour,
This is the tasteless water of Souls—this is the true
           sustenance."

                                        Walt Whitman

Counting waves on the lake. Counting
four mothers, four fathers, five
blonde kids, stars falling out of the sky.

These days are leaving us
They will never be the same.

Boats—and the monotony of boats. Two
kinds of pies. Peach cobbler. Ice
cream. Saying: Please. Saying: Thank
you, or saying what you
have to say with loathsome words. Everyone
talking at once—or not talking
—in accusation, in apology. I'm
sorry. Say you're deeply sorry, and then
try to wash it down with laughter. You must
try to wash it down with laughter between
small sips of afternoon coffee, or between
the sound of small hands, small feet
because these days are leaving us.

Faces in the yellow electric light. Faces
in their books. All the faces that will
rise and fall in your dreams
years from now. Years from now you'll
see their delighted faces as they
open their gifts: the silver
necklace, Chilean verses, wide
brim straw hat, ten dollars towards
the children's rocking chairs. Years
from now you'll watch their hands
folding back the tropical print
wrapping paper, as the lights
go down, as you recount
each one's smile, each
whisper, sky full of exploding
stars, each wave
moving against the break-water.

These days are leaving us.
These days will never be the same.

LETTER OF THANKS TO THE INCOMPORABLE DOCTOR BROTHER BODHISATTVA MEHRDAD MASSOUDI

"And I know that the spirit of God is the eldest brother of my own..."
Walt Whitman

On this freezing cold night the wind has come up
howling from the lands of the hordes, and the snow
is piled higher than the doors and windows of this
pitiful log house, but I want you to know
      I am warm inside the lambs' wool sweater
your mother made with her delicate Persian
hands—the great white sweater with the strong
shoulders and the corded braids across the chest

      —a temple of a sweater, or a pale forest
of a thousand trees—the distinguished white
sweater made with the eight intelligent white
buttons—the brave sweater I am wearing on this
freezing cold night as I fearlessly gallop
across the desert, I am laughing at the spears
and arrows of innumerable Philistine foul
winded armies of lies, deceit, and cultural
decrepitude—because I am wearing the invincible
sweater of no defeat nor surrender.

      Made by the hundred hands of the kindest
woman for her straight-backed strong-hearted
son—named after the great Persian king, whose
status I somehow share inside this soft Persian
      ocean of place and time. On this freezing cold
night, I am warm—even as I write to you—even
as I remain, sincerely, faithfully, your brother
always, as you have always faithfully remained mine.

Song of the Universal

~~Space.~~

<u>Come</u>, said the Muse,
Sing me a song no poet yet has chanted,
Sing me the "Universal.

＃

In this broad Earth of ours,
Amid the measureless grossness & the slag,
Enclosed & safe within its central heart,
Nestles the seed Perfection.

＃

By every life a share, or more or less,
None born but it is born - conceal'd or
　　　　unconceal'd the seed is waiting.

＃

2

Lo! keen-eyed, towering Science!
As from tall peaks the Modern overlooking,
Successive absolute fiats issuing.

＃

47

Yet again, lo! the "Soul—above all Science;
For it, ~~the Soul~~, has ~~entire~~ History gathered
        like husks around the globe;
For it, ~~the Soul~~, the ^entire^ star myriads roll through
        the sky.

                #

In spiral roads, by long detours,
(As a much-tacking ship upon the sea,)
For it, the ~~Real~~ partial to the permanent flowing,
For it, the Real to the Ideal tends.
                #

For it, the mystic evolution;
Not the right only justified—what we call evil
        also justified.

                #

Forth from their masks, no matter what,
From the huge, festering trunk—from craft and
        ^guile & tears,^
Health to emerge, & joy—joy universal.

                #

IN DREAMS PAUL RETURNS TO TELL US WHAT IT'S LIKE

"The armies of those I love engirth me and I engirth them…"
Walt Whitman

I was an insomniac, sleeping like the dead. Bare feet. Cold
sand. I was humming a ragtime tune, the ocean
was making some noise out in the fog, saying
"Come over here and I'll chew your bones." Wind
standing my hair on end, and then a head rises
just above the tide line.

"Hello, Jim."

The head looks like an ice cream-white
hat manikin, but the voice is certainly Paul's.

Already I'm thinking, look, I'm an insomniac
and I'm dreaming for once. I don't want anything
psychological. I want an epic action-movie dream. I want
to grow gills and live underwater in a sunken
tugboat. I want to ride a caped bottlenose dolphin
into cannon fodder, save the Kingdom of the Seals. But no

I get Paul, the guy who watched cervical
cancer disappear his wife in four months, the guy
who put his very-generous trust fund up his nose, the guy
who froze to death on the street full of Bud Lite and Valium
on the coldest night of the year.

"Hello Jim," Paul says again, sounding amazingly chipper
for a man who died with his face frozen to a heat grate. I answer.

49

"Paul, I thought you were dead." Obviously, I never know what to say

"Do I look dead?" he says.

Truth is, he does not look good. The head
is more like an idea of a head, but melted a little. Edvard Munch without
the scream. Something you and your friends wouldn't want
to stumble upon in the dark. I choose not to answer the question.

"Are you playing any music?"

Somewhere there's laughter. The sea inside the fog says, "Come
over here and I'll send in a wave—crush your spine."

"Yeah, Man," says Paul. "I play with Roy Boy Orbison and George. Harrison.
The quiet Beatle. Everyday. Sometimes we tour. Roy Boy taught me how to
roll my R's and holler 'Mercy.'"

I'm thinking pretty good for a guy who just knew how to collect
priceless vintage guitars and change strings.

Then suddenly I feel it: the dream slipping away, traffic noise outside
my window. Charles Dickens and the Ghost of Christmas
Past. The ocean whispers "Not much time left. Right
now. Come over here and we'll make your bones into marble."
                                                  So I
focus on the white head and feel the question rise
out of the tangle of my stomach, rise

                        through my throat, push against
the back of my front teeth until I say it.

"Paul, what is it like?"

More laughter out of nowhere. Paul speaks.

"Well, actually, it's a lot like Puerto Rico—the winter we stayed
on the beach. Every day it was 85, and one night Eileen and I take
the boat out—it's against the rules—the landlady telling us
there are hungry, razor teeth in these waters, things bigger
than a house, lurking, down deep, waiting for you, food
chain—but we row out anyway into the starry, starry night, the oars
banging, so Eileen takes off her shirt, shorts and purple
underwear. We wrap and muffle those oars in her clothes. Drift
on a flat sea for hours, every once in a while see a flash
of phosphorescence, something big down there moving
around. Dark though. Can't see her in the inside-of-a-horse
darkness of it all. Silver and gold lights make a necklace
bead line on the Puerto Rico coast.
                           I reach out, can't find her, but I know she's
there. Hear her breathing. Think all my life I've wanted
to love someone like this, and now I do, think I could sing
her body electric
                      feel the pressure
on my heart like it's some bloody water balloon
in free-fall. Jumping-out-of-a-plane freefalling
into your great-great-great-great grandmother's arms.

What's it like? It's a lot like that.

WALT WHITMAN'S LETTER OF THANKS AFTER SKATING ALL AFTERNOON AT THE DUKE NELSON MEMORIAL HOCKEY ARENA

Today, Duke, the little dark circles of ice inside
everyone's heart collectively unite under
extensive fluorescent illumination
—and, of course, your ever-present heavenly
gaze. Our Duke. Old Duke, who art
in heaven—the beloved hockey coach
renowned for playing favorites and denying
nothing—which in itself is
undeniable on an afternoon where the whole

town skates in a circle holding
hands, or on an afternoon where the reproductive
sons and daughters of a town plucked
out of a Bergman movie arrive with their life-
size Barbie and Ken dolls and skate
counter-clockwise in earthly
rotation, weaving through the intricate
patterns of togetherness and personal
agenda, left and right, so many little
drops of blood, Duke. I mean, really, you should
see them, heavy-footed, swarming all over
the ice, or on the team bench where the old
men in their baggy pants blow out
plumes of white breath—the same
color as the overhead lights, which always
makes me wonder what the stuff is
made out of anyway—breath—light. Is it
the same, or do you know, Duke? I mean, is it

all made clear somehow? Do you get a little
boost of IQ with discarnation? Regardless, today

I'm cutting smooth ice into fine snow, gliding
deep into the corners, my skates
skittering a little behind, face going red
to pale, cold sweat inside my intrepid freedom
red, white, and blue flying-duck sweater, a burst
of speed down the straights, and when I look up
the whole town's grinning moon-faced in love, and I'm
about to shout: Hey. Everybody. I'm Walt
Whitman on ice—a situation pushing you ever
upward in the standings, Our Duke, hallowed
be thy name. Even in your present condition you have
die-hard fans, and another season where you are, once
again, miraculously and posthumously undefeated.

PHOTOGRAPH OF MY PARENTS AT THE SPRING FORMAL—1949

"Allons! out of the dark confinement!
It is useless to protest—I know all, and expose it.
Behold through you as bad as the rest!
Through the laughter, dancing, dining, supping, of people,
Inside of dresses and ornaments, inside of those wash'd
        and trimm'd faces,
Behold a secret silent loathing and despair!"

                                        Walt Whitman

The story drops down. The moon rises. When the royal
cook turns her back to feed the royal orange
cat, a long, tall stranger slips into the castle
strong. Look out: he's caped, daggered, his sword
swings deep in the veneer of a swagger he lifted
from an Errol Flynn movie, and as he slides
down the black corridor towards the music and laughter
his heart tells him: Tonight will be the night.

Her heart tells her to leave for the unfinished
Thomas Wolfe novel she's got going. Her heart
tells her to go to the everlasting dorm
bridge game, or even to capitalize on a little
of that beauty sleep, of which she needs none.
Regardless, she stands vibrating inside the peach
chiffon gown her grandmother bought for her
birthday, unaware that boys in this very room
would later die on the Korean peninsula with her
name on their lips, or age away in heartland

obscurity after making a pile in the lumber
business, dreaming of the night they box-stepped
with a goddess.

                    And in a roomful of young, immaculate
dragon-slayers, captains courageous, knights
of code and honor, the irony of the ages settles
around her and cloaks her sight: By midnight
she chooses her man, and the hand she holds
in the photograph becomes the hand that would slip
rings around her fingers, stroke her long golden
hair, hold her children
                    —but it would also be the hand
that would blacken her eyes, break her bones, the hand
that would lead her deep into the kingdoms of darkness
and break her, piece by piece, until the photograph
becomes someone else's story, a cautionary tale
told in the evening to keep wayward children
close to the lamplight and fire, or nightmarish
fevering in their blankets.
                    Fifty years later, the picture's
still telling the same story. Fifty years later they're
still so unbelievably beautiful they could decorate
every night in oblivion, two reeling diamonds
tumbling in the darkness dusk to dawn, holding hands
forever unable to let each other go.

GRANDMA, THE ROBBER, AND THE BLUE RAINBOW WALL

The night Grandma got robbed, she was reading her old leather-bound book, and watching *Little House on the Prairie*. It was her favorite TV show because it reminded her so much of growing up on Big Cottonwood, the Hendrickson ranch in North Dakota.

"Every day, you never knew what was going to happen on the ranch. One morning I came down to breakfast, and there were six Indian women and two men sitting around our table drinking coffee, and eating eggs and ham. Everybody was laughing, and my mother was speaking a language I couldn't understand. She was speaking Sioux. They all sure made a big fuss over me. I was three years old, and I found out later that all those people were relatives. One man scooped me up, and I had my breakfast on his lap. He was my great grandfather, Turtle Man. He had made me a pair of beaded elk hide moccasins—with the fur inside. Jimmy, they were so warm and beautiful. I felt like a princess when I wore them. My mother had to make me take them off when I took a bath, and I cried and cried."

Her smile broke across her face, and she closed her eyes. From across a room, everything she said sounded like the rhythm and blues of the *Canterbury Tales*, Middle English, and not that she owed anything to Geoffrey Chaucer. She came by it honestly, did her own pilgrimages on the prairie.

"It was a hard life for my parents, our closest neighbors were six miles away, and hard things happened, but we loved it. I always felt so loved."

She'd purse her lips together and flash me a little smile. She was ninety-nine years old, which seemed like a miracle in itself, but even at ninety-nine with her deep snowy hair, it was easy to imagine her as a little pink-haired girl in the same green gingham dress. Maybe the only difference was that she had traded in her puppy's belly face for a road map around her mouth and eyes, and those creases were deep from years of laughing.

Grandma also liked Michael Landon, who played Pa Ingalls on *Little House*. Michael Landon reminded her of her Uncle Christian, who had wavy dark hair, played the fiddle, and had a great way with animals. He also loved to dance.

"One Sunday afternoon Uncle Christian came over and taught me. He said, 'Step on my feet, Little Squeaky,' his arms wide. He called me Squeak, said I was a squeaky little mouse. I stepped on his feet, and he twirled me around the kitchen humming the Kristiania Waltz. His beard was so long, I could feel it bobbing on top my head. I didn't dare look up. He never married. No woman would have him. I don't think the world made a kinder or a homelier man, but ten minutes later, I knew how to waltz."

She squeezed her eyes shut. I started to think that there was a TV going on inside her head, and I wished I could watch it with her.

The night Grandma got robbed, there was a blizzard on the TV movie of *Little House*, and there was a blizzard in Milwaukee, Wisconsin, the day before, and the day before that. It was a light, crunchy, icy snow, single digits, blowing banshee off Lake Michigan, gusts up to sixty miles per hour, sometimes rattling the windows and shaking the old bones of her tiny bungalow. The power had been off for about a day, but Grandma was cozy. She had flipped the switch on the diesel generator my grandfather had rigged up before he died; she had laid a small fire in the Glenwood H cook stove my grandfather had buffaloed into her kitchen over seventy years ago, and she had her mother's wool quilt spread over her knees.

She said the man appeared in the circle of blue TV light and sat down in the same over-stuffed rocker I was sitting in. He was dressed in black, except he was covered in snow. It was way past midnight.

"I didn't hear you knock," my grandmother said.

"I didn't knock. I took your storm door apart and let myself in. I need some money."

"Was he big, Grandma? Was he black? Maybe he was Mexican? Was he Puerto Rican? Part of the Islamic immigrant community?"

"Yes, he was big, and he sounded like you."

"Me?"

Grandma nodded and leaned back in her own over-stuffed blue Naugahyde rocker.

"I told him so, too. 'You sound like my grandson, Jimmy.' But he just sat right there in your grandfather's chair, not moving, staring, like a dog getting ready to bite."

She pointed at my face like I was someone else. I couldn't believe how small her fingers were.

"'I need some money, white woman,' he said."

"So he was black, Grandma."

"I don't know. It was dark in the room, just the TV, and Michael Landon, Pa Ingalls I mean, was trying to harness his team of horses, loading up to go into town. It was a perfectly fine day, balmy for January 12th, but the horses were having none of it. Very uncharacteristically, they were fighting him—broke loose, ran back to their stalls. Stomped, reared, you name it, Jimmy. Those horses knew."

She laughed and put her hand to her face, shook her head, and started rocking. I watched her look up at the crystal candelabra hanging from her ceiling. The prisms were catching the morning light and casting small rainbows across her huge TV and the light blue wall full of photographs.

"Those horses already knew a killer blizzard was on the way, even though it was warm and clear, but the people didn't, so Pa saddled-up Sassy Britches, the Indian pony Standing Bear had given him. The United States Army Signal Corps was put in place to warn people about the weather, but they took the day off, I guess. Pa had to pay his mortgage on time or lose the farm, and he needed to pick up some medicine for a neighbor's child who was deathly ill. Things were always going wrong for those Ingalls. I put the show on pause so I wouldn't miss anything. It was one of my favorites. My parents lived through that storm, the Children's Blizzard of '88. So did I."

"You knew which blizzard it was?"

"Of course, Jimmy. Everybody my age knows about it. Just about everybody in North Dakota lost someone. My best friend and her sisters died."

I watched her face fall for a second, and she looked at the wall of people to the right of the TV, but she came right back up.

"But what about the robber, Grandma?"

"Yes, well, I told him, 'I'm sorry but I'm not all white. My mother was half Yankton Sioux.'"

I felt weightless for a moment, those seconds when you launch yourself off the high-dive, everything's going all right, and then your belly finds the flat water.

"We're Yankton Sioux?"

She nodded hard at the surprise in my voice and started what I'd have to call her accelerated giggle.

"Oh, yes, we're Yankton. So much of the family thinks we're all

Norwegians from Telemark, but it's not quite true. You know, Jimmy, there was a lot of fucking back then."

I tried to disguise the heave in my chest, but she wasn't stupid; she saw it and threw her head back laughing. I was still in my mid-twenties, and if I ever think about it now, I sure didn't know much, but I did know how to keep my mouth shut. And I knew when somebody said something that you should never forget, all you have to do is lay down a book marker in your mind, and you'll be able to come back for it whenever you need to. I watched her stroke the quilt a few times with her left hand, like she was trying to smooth something out. Woolen horses were running across a woolen prairie. There were big trees, buffalo, and the Little Missouri River. A woolen little girl was holding hands with a woolen Indian. Both of us had ear-to-ear grins.

"So did you give the robber money?"

"Yes, I did, but it wasn't easy. I told him to go upstairs to the front bedroom and get my green alligator wallet out of the top left dresser drawer. 'You go get it,' he said. That's when I told him, 'I'm ninety-nine. I don't go upstairs anymore. If you want some money, you're going to have to go get it yourself.' I felt like I was speaking to your father when he was a boy—or a man. Jimmy, your father gave us trouble as soon as he arrived. It's like he popped out of the womb with a cigarette in one hand and a bottle of whiskey in the other."

We both laughed, but her face flattened out a little, and I watched her look at the black wooden plate my grandfather had mounted on the wall over seventy years ago that read: Gi oss i dag vårt daglige brød. It took me over ten years, but I came to understand that every family has someone like my father. Every family has that person with a history of miraculous escapes, close calls, and people looking the other way until the luck runs out. My father was driving home drunk for the three-thousandth time in a bad storm. Cops told us he died instantly in the crash. My brother, however, hung on for a couple of days.

Grandma cleared her throat, I watched her face get stony for a moment, but then she came bobbing up like an apple. I'll never understand how some people are wired. Doesn't matter how many times you throw them down or they get bucked off. Next thing you know, they're back on their feet, dancing. Then there's that other crew who are always looking for ways to fall. Just don't get it.

"What did he do?" I asked her, and she cocked her head at me, squinted her eyes. "The robber, I mean."

"He went upstairs, but he told me if I tried to use the telephone, he'd kill me."

She gave me a pronounced nod when she said it, something you might do when you shake somebody's hand after a business agreement. Now-the-farm's-yours sort of thing. Handshake. Nod.

"My God, Grandma, you must have been terrified."

She shook her head side to side in definitive tennis match style. Twenty years later I'd watch Portuguese, Chinese, and Indian old women shake their heads in the same way. Portuguese old women would shake their heads and spit on the ground. There was no equivocation: the answer was no—in Universal Grandmother.

"Oh no. I don't know why, but I wasn't. 'Underneath a big pair of blue and red woolen socks,' I told him. He did. He went up and got the wallet, and I could hear him move so carefully, gently opened and closed the dresser drawer. When he came downstairs, he handed me the wallet, just like I told him. Over the last two years, I had saved a little more than eighty dollars from my check. I took it out and handed it to him. It was a huge handful of small bills. And then I told him, 'Here, I want you to have this. I can see you're a good man. You just need some money.' When he reached for it in the TV light of Michael Landon's frozen smile, I could also see the holes in his black pants and coat. His face was sweating, and his hands shook. And did he smell like sour milk. Yes, he took the money, looked at it in the TV light, then at me, put his hands over his face and started to cry."

"He did what?" I could feel my face get red, a wave of something coming up from my chest, throat, cheeks. Whatever it was, it was making my ears ring.

"Yes, he started to cry. He put his hands over his face and started to cry. I reached out and held him by the elbow."

"You did what?"

"I reached out, grabbed his elbow and pulled him towards me. He knelt beside my chair, this chair right here, put his face on my lap and cried and cried and cried, like he had fallen off his bike and tore-up his knees on the gravely pavement. This quilt, right here, had a dinner plate-size wet spot."

She lifted the blanket off her knees a little and shook it. Pronounced banker nod. Beautiful full hazel-eye contact.

"I held his head in my lap. 'It's all right,' I told him. 'Everything's going to be all right. Don't you worry now.' 'I'm so sorry, ma'am,' he said. 'I'm sorry. I'm sorry. I'm sorry. It's the crack.'"

"So Grandma, you had a crying crack addict in your lap who had threatened to kill you? You know about crack?"

Her face beamed in the light again, and for a moment I saw her as the high-stepping three-year-old on everybody's lap bouncing from knee to knee, the young girl galloping across the prairie on her black and white pony. She looked at me hawk-eyed, rocked a little more deliberately in her chair, and then motioned with her eyes to a picture on the wall. It was my grandfather in his World War I uniform with his arm around another soldier.

"Your grandfather's best friend, Marten Christofferson, came back from France a morphine addict. He had battle fatigue, too. If a pot dropped in the kitchen, he'd be on the floor, shaking, wet his pants. It took him over a year on the ranch with some good food and family, doing something with his hands besides killing people. Marten had a gift with animals. Yes, it took him a year, and he was our boy again. Never could stand loud noise though. When tractors came in, Marten stuck with his beautiful black mules. Yes, Jimmy, I know all about crack. Old people know everything. No one thinks we do, but we do."

She looked back at the picture. Shook her head. I could almost see both my grandfather and Marten underneath the prism rainbows.

"You know Marten asked me to marry him? Your grandfather's best friend. We were walking back from the Lutheran church, and he told me he just really didn't like Indians, said they were dirty and you couldn't trust them, and I told him, 'Marten Christofferson, you're going to have to find yourself somebody else to have your babies.' There are some men in this world that would be a lot better off if they kept their mouths permanently shut so they don't reveal just how stupid they are."

Little girl laugh. Three years old.

"So Grandma, what happened with the robber?"

"I rocked him a little and he settled down. Being so close, though, the smell was pretty bad, so I told him he had to go upstairs and take a shower."

She watched my eyes get big, her smile getting bigger.

"Yes, I told him he had to go upstairs and take a shower. And I told him he'd find some clean clothes in your father's yellow room. 'Be sure to put on some long underwear, and you'll find my son's Navy issue blue jeans up there, some sweaters, and there's a red buffalo plaid hunting coat. There's a good pair of winter boots up there, too, and be sure to take those blue and red wool socks where the wallet was. And there's a razor up there, don't you know. I bet you have a face under all that fur.' 'Yes, ma'am,' he said. Very polite boy. Sweet boy. Just like you, Jimmy."

Felt my teeth clench hard in my face—then go slack.

"What did he do?"

"Jimmy, no one can argue with an old lady. Twenty minutes later he was back downstairs carrying his old clothes, and that was all the time I needed to make some ham and eggs. The stove was already hot."

"You fed the robber, Grandma?"

"Of course I fed him. On his way upstairs, I said to him, 'I know what you are.' I pointed my finger right at him, too, and he froze there right on the steps, turned at me, lowered his shoulders like I had just hit him. Almost started to cry again. 'I know what you are. You're hungry,' I told him. I know when a man's hungry. All the time."

She pushed down hard with her feet, threw her head back. Now, I thought, *Grandma, you could be one of those three witches in* Macbeth—*or maybe all three.*

"What did he do?"

"He nodded his head and kept on going, maybe a little faster. Yes, I sat him down in your grandfather's chair with a TV tray, with six eggs, ham, a short stack of pancakes, good Wisconsin maple syrup, and some strong Norwegian coffee."

And I sure knew what that was. Stuff could tan a deer hide. I was drinking some while disappearing most of the krumkaker she brought out for me. After a while, you feel like you've been shot out of a cannon. If you have straight hair, Norwegian coffee will curl it. If your hair's curly, that coffee will make your hair fall out. Grandma's world did not include decaf.

Somewhere around now her blue TV room started to spin a little bit, disco style, in the prism light. It was full of mules and morphine, the smell of good dirt, cow ponies, and Yankton Sioux. My grandmother sat there rocking away, watching me almost swoon in it all, little girl smile on her face. Then something occurred to me. Somewhere in between all the fucking, all the love, hate, pain, regret, and death, these people were having a lot of fun. I started to wish I could have been with them. Then she brought me back.

"When I put down the food in front of him, he hung his head, and his hands were shaking almost too much to hold a knife and fork."

"What did he say?"

"He didn't say anything. He held on to his fork and knife and ate that plate of food like he had never eaten before in his life. I just let him work on it."

Amplified, accelerated giggle.

"Men always turn animal when it comes to food. It's so funny. Women would be better off if they lived with cave dogs, or bears, or saber-toothed tigers. I spun the video back to the beginning so Charles would have an idea of what's going on."

"His name was Charles?"

"Yes, I told Charles that Pa had to go to town to pay the mortgage, or they were going to lose the farm, and he needed to pick up some serum for a neighbor boy who was dying. On top of it all, a snow storm was coming up. Killer blizzard."

"What did Charles say?"

"He just nodded and kept on eating, said, 'Pa better be careful.' So once he saddles-up the Indian pony, everything goes OK for Pa on the way there, but the storm's coming, and nobody knows it. It's the Blizzard of 1888. The banker is clearly disappointed that Pa pays the mortgage on time, but the doctor has the serum ready for the dying neighbor boy. Trouble is, by the time Pa heads back, it's all white-out, the temperature has dropped down to forty below zero. It's a white gale. And the blizzard of 1888 did all that—and more. The wind comes up and knocks Pa clear off the Indian pony. He's lost in the snow. He can't see, the snow is as fine as sifted flour, his eyes are iced shut, but the pony nuzzles him, and he's able to get back on to his feet. It's too windy to ride, so Pa grabs the pony's tail and just follows. The pony takes him to Standing Bear's village."

"What's Charles doing during all this?"

"Charles woke up around the time Pa fell off his horse."

"Your robber fell asleep?"

Grandma did her definitive nod and wiggled her entire body, all five feet of it, back into the blue cloud of her rocker.

"Your grandfather's chair. Gets them every time."

"What kind of shape was Standing Bear in?"

"Oh they were all perfectly snug in their earth lodges, their animals were well sheltered and fed, kids all asleep under buffalo robes. But Standing Bear hears the pony and goes out in the storm and brings Pa in to thaw out and get something to eat. In North Dakota, the Yankton were always saving us. In the Children's Blizzard, during the early morning, it was almost thirty degrees bright and sunny, and Turtle Man comes galloping up to our ranch and tells my mother not to send us to school, tells her she just has a couple of hours before a blizzard comes, tells her if we don't protect our animals, they will die. My mother said he called the storm 'White Death.' My father only knew a few words of Sioux and Turtle Man only knew a few words of English, but by the time he galloped away, my parents were just racing around like the world was going to end. And it was, too. Around 3:00 in the afternoon it sounded like a locomotive was coming across the prairie, looked like a huge black wave. Dropped over four feet of snow, drifts fifty feet high. The Indians were always saving the white people. That's what no one seems to know anymore."

She shook her head and glanced down at her quilt. All around the woolen figures, hundreds of small white tuffs of wool were scattered across the blue background.

"So Grandma, what happened to Pa?"

"Pa eats and then drinks something hot, but tells Standing Bear that he has to deliver the serum to the neighbor family. The storm is raging outside, and it's clear Pa can't handle it. Standing Bear rummages around and pulls out two pairs of snow shoes, throws on his buffalo coat, and the two set off together in the Maelstrom."

"In the what, Grandma?"

"Maelstrom, Jimmy. An exceedingly powerful whirlpool, a term usually reserved for the sea—or a river. I'm using the word figuratively." Banker face. She never let people who weren't on her level feel like they were idiots. "Right. A maelstrom. Now, what's Charles doing?"

"Charles was rocking along with me. He just said, 'I hope Standing Bear knows what he's doing, because Pa doesn't have the good sense the Lord gave him.'"

"What did you say?"

"Well, Charles was right, of course. Standing Bear ties a rope around Pa and leads him to the neighbor's door; however, Pa does his best not to make it."

"The neighbor boy lives?"

"Yes, the neighbor boy lives, but Pa won't stay the night there. He says he needs to go back and protect his family from the storm—so out they go again."

"This sounds a little off to me, Grandma."

"Yes, of course it's off. But the two of them go out again in the blizzard, Standing Bear leading the way, rope around Pa, and Pa's trying to find a way to die the entire time. He almost walks over a cliff, starts heading down into the Little Missouri River, falls down exhausted. Charles was right: clearly, Pa has no sense."

"Grandma, is there a storm that could do that?"

Her face got rocky again, steel-cut eyes, and then fell a little bit. On the pine wall in back of her chair was a family portrait. Six kids lined up in a row, standing behind a man and a woman, who were seated in ornate wooden chairs. There was a toddler on the man's knee, and that little girl clearly was screaming while everybody else was smiling away. Two of the boys on the ends were holding horses on lead lines, and in the background was a beautiful dove-tailed log house with a wrap-around porch. The screamer was my grandmother.

"Our neighbors lost most of their herd. The next spring, they found frozen steers in the limbs of trees, drifts were so high. Fifty feet. Bad things can happen, Jimmy. My best girlfriend froze to death on her way home."

She looked up again at the black wooden plate on the wall and shook her head.

"A lot of kids died coming back from school, and some kids made it. My best friend Jenny Henderson died in that storm with her sisters. Her parents found all four of them together in a snow drift. Their arms were locked around each other, trying to keep each other warm. They suffered so."

There was a hard silence, and like always, I didn't know what to say. Finally, we both came up for air.

"Well Grandma, Pa makes it back, right?"

"Well, of course he makes it back, and falls on his face right on the cabin floor. His wife, Caroline, comes running with Charles Jr. in her arms, and then Mary, Carrie, Grace—Cassandra and Albert and James—the three adopted children, and the fire's bright, and everybody's happy, and while Pa's hugging everybody he's saying, 'Thank God Almighty, Thank the Lord, Thank God, God, God, God, God,' and it just makes me mad."

I watched her hands rolling into little fists. Anvil jaw.

"What he needed to say was, 'Thank Standing Bear.' Pa, thank your Indian friend Standing Bear who led you through the storm and saved the life of the neighbor boy, and brought you home safely to your family, but it never occurs to Pa. That's the problem with Pa: there's just too much God. I'm just not all that fond on God. I like the people. Ma was hugging Pa, the kids came down from the loft, and everybody was hugging everybody else—and what about Standing Bear? Pa turns around, and Standing Bear has already left, leaving Pa a beautiful pair of snowshoes. Nobody's worried about the Indian getting back home. Standing Bear had miles more to go through that killer storm. I think God just got in Pa's way."

I felt like my whole body was going to explode out of my whole body.

"What did Charles say about it?"

"Oh, he just laughed and shook his head. Charles and I both agreed that Standing Bear was our favorite in the show. 'Now there's a man,' said Charles."

"But Grandma, you went to church your entire life, you go to church now—and you don't believe in God?"

"I didn't say that. I'm just saying that I've always loved churches, the buildings, even the good clean smell of them when we were kids. And I love the music, the hymns, and the singing, and the food, and the people, our neighbors; some of them you wouldn't want to be in the same room with outside of Sunday."

She reached over to the side of her rocker where there was

a wide wooden slot my grandfather had attached that held yarn and knitting needles; and underneath it all, she pulled out a book, waved an ancient leather bound edition of *Leaves of Grass* in my face. The leather cover was well-cracked and stained, and it looked like there were more than twenty pieces of ribbon marking pages.

"It's his so-called 'Death Bed Edition,'" she said. "Do you know Walt? He worked on this book for his entire writing life, got it just the way he wanted, and then he died. He was a gay homosexual, applauded and ridiculed. Even today people can't make up their minds about him."

Banker nod. Somebody just bought a farm.

"You read Walt Whitman?" But I don't think she heard me. When things get really strange, you just have to try to keep your mouth shut.

"So Grandma, what about Charles? How did it all end?"

"Well, it was about 4:00 or so, I guess. Still black and blowing. Charles put my storm door back together, said he attached the glass from the inside so nobody could ever break into the house that way. And he shoveled out my porch, stoop, and walk, and then I watched him disappear into the storm. That blizzard would hang on until mid-morning. I hated to think about Charles out there."

I sat rocking in my grandfather's chair waiting for her to say something. In the prism light of her mother's lamp, I thought she had fallen asleep, but she started to rock again, book in her lap. She opened her eyes, stopped rocking, full hazel-eyed contact. I had no idea at the time what she was saying, but about a year later, after I discovered that she had stuffed her *Leaves of Grass* in a brown paper bag under the driver's seat of my truck, I realized that she was quoting from Whitman's "Drum-Taps."

"One turns to me his appealing eyes—poor boy! I never knew you, yet I think I could not refuse this moment to die for you, if that could save you."

She lifted her head and scanned the people on the blue rainbow wall, like she was checking in with every single one of them, my grandfather, Uncle Christian, Jenny, Marten and his mules, my great-grandmother and Turtle Man.

"How I miss talking to you, Jimmy. Wish so much you had grown up around here. Your father kept you boys away from us. We could have had so much fun."

I knew that was true, too, and I told her so, and then I got to work, which was why I stopped in the first place. I took off her storm windows, stacked them neatly up in the garage attic along with the glass panel in the front door that the robber came through. Put on her screens. I swept her front porch; scraped, and painted it barn red; made a dump run; and then I mowed and raked her back lawn. Those old bungalows had huge back yards for being in town. You could step out back, and feel like you're on the edge of the prairie—almost.

It must have been when I was mowing that she planted her book in my truck. Sometimes I try to imagine her stealing out of that house without me seeing her with that floaty walk she had, moving like she was an inch or two in the air everywhere she went. I don't know how she did it, but after all, she was, in part, Yankton Sioux. The inscription on the cover page was written in the most elegant handwriting: "For our Irene, who is in love with the world, on her sixteenth birthday. February 27, 1901." It was signed "Mother and Daddy." Right below it was another inscription: "For my grandson Jimmy. Remember me."

When it was time to go, she sprang to her feet like a kitten, forced forty dollars into my pocket, taking the money out of her green alligator wallet. I told her I felt like a robber, both of us laughing all over again.

When she walked me to my truck, we went out the kitchen back door and into the pole wood shed my grandfather had built onto the house in the 30s. She still had over two cords of wood stacked up for her cook stove. The diesel generator was out there with the exhaust cleverly vented out the metal roof, and my grandfather's green plaid hunting clothes were hanging from a ten-point deer rack.

When we got to my truck, she reached up and grabbed my face with her two tiny hands, pulled me down and gave me a giant wet kiss on the cheek—and then another. She smelled like lilac, lavender, and ham. With those two tiny hands she squeezed my cheeks and drew me down, again, close to her face, and then said it, almost in a whisper.

"What will you do, Jimmy? What will you do when your children are lost out in the storm?"

She was almost one-hundred then, and she'd live for another year and a half. I drove across the country to graduate school that fall to get my fine arts degree.

I never saw her again.

An Epistolary Reconnection With The Old Man

"These are the days that must happen to you…"

Walt Whitman

The other day, I smelled your breath
on the breath of some drunken
fool—a friend of my wife's—and I
imagined you rising

                out of your grave
in front of that 250 year old Congregational
Church in suburban Pennsylvania

                        checking

out the lay of the land, and then
walking, of course, walking on the trail
of all the lost, wandering spirits—

                     thousands
of them, I imagined—all of you trying to find
your way home to make it right.

                     I imagined you
—walking the highways, passing through whining
Japanese look-a-like cars, smoking diesels
—walking, relentless—

              through lovers, drunk
Saturday night making kids—walking

                     —and then
maybe you see somebody like yourself, beating
the shit out of his wife and boys

                  —and then crying, of course
—crying lakes and rivers for it, crying

head down at the bus station for it

                                —crying

across bitter root mountains, white bone
desert, making an ocean—seven seas maybe.

I even imagined you showing up some night
at my door, all ghostly, reverentially
apologetic, full of wishes, revision, make
believe. So let's

                        make believe. Let's
make you knock at my door, make me
happy to see you, let you in, take your
shoes, sit you down in a chair
by the stove, and tell you everything
that's become of me. And let's

                            make believe
you are listening as I tell you I am habitually
followed through the streets by an entourage
of smiling dogs and giggling children, fawned-eyed
crazies, by the beautiful

                      —compassionate
—by the exuberant, by the howling
mad

      —and then let's make believe that this is
somehow because of you

                    —because it is. Do
you hear me?

              I will sit you in that stuffed
chair by the stove all night until
the marrow in your bones is warm again—until
your eyes open wide in the light of day. That's

right. You could stay all night if you like
—and in the morning, I'd serve you tea. Can

you hear me? Can you brush the dirt
out of your ears? Can you put
your ear to the door or to all the doors
that have closed on you? Listen:

It's all right. Be well. Rest in peace.

JUMPING JIM'S POETRY EMERGENCY

"I think heroic deeds were all conceiv'd in the open air, and all great poems also;
I think I could stop here myself, and do miracles;
(My judgments, thoughts, I henceforth try by the open air, the road;)
I think whatever I shall meet on the road I shall like, and whoever beholds me
shall like me;
I think whoever I see must be happy."

Walt Whitman

First, you forget what anything
is—you only know
what things are like. Your hair

catches fire, turns white, and stands
on end—while the visions come
copiously, in color, and at least

once or twice a night. And then
the wanderings, the articulate
ramblings, the purchase

of the service revolver. You're forced
to one platitude after
another: starry nights, black moons, full

lips, somebody's exquisite vulnerable
ass, and of course, wine
wine, wine—until you ask:

Is there gas in the truck? And Yes—

there's gas in the truck—so you launch
yourself into high speed expressive

intoxication, leaving a trail of blue
lights, until it's the end
of the road for Jumping

Jim and his dog, Woe. You've
arrived—and with only one
credible explanation:

Your Honor, I'm afraid
there's been a poetry emergency.

THE UPWARDLY MOBILE LITTLE CITY SELECTMEN INTENSIFY THEIR INVESTIGATION OF NATURE BOY

"Listen! I will be honest with you,
I do not offer the old smooth prizes, but offer rough new prizes,
These are the days that must happen to you:
You shall not heap up what is call'd riches,
You shall scatter with lavish hand all that you earn or achieve…"

Walt Whitman

We went down to his house and shouted his Christian
name in the air, but afterwards—nothing—not
a sound, so we prowled around his magnificent
pile of pre-war Fords, pulled some parts, smashed a few
headlights to see if, this way, we might get his
attention. When that didn't work, we banged
hard on every window of his house until
one of them shattered and let us in
past the ragged curtain—shooing every deranged
cow bird and red squirrel out of the place.
Animals in, animals out, we thought. And then we

walked around for a while, speculating
on the unmade bed, the ancient gold framed
picture of his dead wife, the dog-haired
easy-chair, not to mention a rather artistic
display of track and football trophies on his
splintering oak bureau covered with a couple
hundred year of mouse turds and bird shit. We
even speculated on why he lies
naked in the November sun, and why he

lives off wild berries and hickory nuts, why he
trots along the side of the road wearing almost
nothing—a little brown man floating along
wrapped in a diaper. We walked around his
house speculating on these matters. We
walked around wanting to talk to him, hoping
he might explain a few things, but he wasn't
there, and it didn't look like he'd
arrive any time soon, so we all

left by the front door, and when we did, the door
flew off its hinges and fell apart in our
hands. But that's OK, we thought. This way
he'll know we came to see him, that we
hung around for a while—waiting. He'll
know he has something we want, and he'll know
one of these fine days, we'll be back to get it.

Back On The Ghost Road

"Not I, nor anyone else can travel that road for you,
You must travel it for yourself.
It is not far, it is within reach,
Perhaps you have been on it since you were born and did not know.
Perhaps it is every where—on water and land."

Walt Whitman

Re-materialize in the bitter cold—in elemental
variation—rain, wind, snow. You're the man
standing on a hill above the train and tracks. Stone
farm. River. Purple valley. Nine shadow horses
grazing on the night pasture. Or re-materialize

in headlights, motor hum, black road—a wheel
vibrating in your hands. You're the stiff tired
man moving towards a tree-lined house where the dog
won't bark when you pull into the yard, where
the door magically opens for your key—in the rain
and wind, stone steps, yellow porch light, blue
storm door, red cupboards, mail on the kitchen
table unbelievably addressed to you. Or in the middle

of the black dog night the clock ticks backwards until
your numerous significant dead are alive again—and they
move through you like smoke, rise around you, fill
every face in every picture on the wall, while you
sit in a wooden chair that holds your back against
hours and hours, while you read mail from people who'll
crack a smile at the very mention of your name, whoever
you are with the three-toed dog at your feet, or whoever
you've become. Listen. Congratulations. You've made it home.

RIDING LESSON
(First Riding Lesson at Brown's Stables
Lyda J. Brown, Prop.)

"I swear to you there are divine things more beautiful than words can tell."
                                                    Walt Whitman

A horse that rolls is worth a hundred dollars.
A horse with a blue eye is insane.
A horse named after a Confederate general belongs
        in a dog food can, and if you can't
        get him into a can, don't
        worry about it; he'll do it
        all by himself, and if he doesn't
        get around to it, somebody else will.

A horse with a hard mouth is worthless.
A horse that bolts for the barn should be laced
unmercifully, and a horse that won't
stand for a mount or the smith should be
beaten with a shillelagh until that little
light bulb between its ears begins to glow.

A Bay or a Black is worthy of a king, and when
        a king rides, he should hold his head
        high but never haughty.

A horse that's head-shy has been abused by some
        fool, and it's not the beast's fault
        he won't take the bit—
        somebody else should take it for him.

81

And don't you think God doesn't see you, and don't
you think that there aren't
            angels with manes and tails.
And don't you think they won't judge you
the way St. Peter will judge you
when you try to enter the Lord's
Kingdom of Heaven.
            I guarantee
a horse can carry you to heaven, and you'll
arrive.
            Now look me in the eye. The reins
on this beast are the lines into her heart.
You take them, and let this mare know she's yours.

After the Dazzle of Day

After the dazzle of day is gone,
Only the dark dark night shows
    to my eyes the stars;
After the clangor of organ majestic,
    or chorus, or perfect band,
Silent, athwart my soul, moves the
    symphony true.

Walt Whitman

pub. in
~~————~~
early in Feb. '88

83

How Ed And Emma Of The Foggy River Farm Grow Stars

"...I became tired and sick,
Till rising and gliding out I wander'd off by myself,
In the mystical moist night-air, and from time to time,
Look'd up in perfect silence at the stars."

                                    Walt Whitman

There's an old man and an old woman at the back
corner of the market, selling root crops and blue
eggs, ice cold Jersey milk with a three inch
white bubbly head, homemade sweet potato
French fries while you watch, homestead
garlic sauce, Russian black bread, fire red ketchup, eight
inch ginger molasses cookies, blueberry pie.

Ed's the cashier, has milk white eyes and makes
silver change by feel, holds the paper money up
in the air for Emma, who identifies denominations
by founding fathers first names.
                          "That's George, Ed. That's
Alexander. That's Ulysses S., and it looks like he's
blinking. Ulysses don't see the light of day much
in our house, does he, Ed."
                          "No Ma'am, you got
that right."
                  Emma cackles and throws her head back, a purple
scarf swaying under her huge purple eyes, but when she's
still, wild birds land on her hands. Emma's
smile is so big, it could light up the inside
of a pocket.

Little children run by—stop in their tracks, say it
too loud. "Look Momma. At the man's eyes. What's wrong
with his eyes?"

                                Ed laughs between making change. "It's
not that I'm blind," he says. "It's just I can't see."

                                                          And then
somewhere in the hundreds of
transactions, he touches a young woman's hand. "Oh
Emma," he says, nodding deep and long as a bow, nodding
nodding. "Emma. This one, here."

                                                Without a beat, Emma
places a long cylindrical burlap bag in the young
woman's hands, and inside looks to be pebbles, darker
and redder than cherries.

                                      "You must eat one every
day," says Emma. "Little by little, your sight will change."

                And the young woman eats, eyes wide and watery
flush on her cheeks, smile spreading at the corners of her mouth.

"My god," she says. "Delicious. What are these? I don't think I've ever
had anything so delicious in my entire life."

"Star seeds," says Emma. "A rare thing indeed. Now, you'll know
what the stars know. But only Ed can choose. You see, a star
child must first have a true, brave heart."

"I see," the young woman said. "Yes, I can see," she said rising
into the sky. "I can see so far. I can see."

And in this way many star children have come into our world. Theylight up the night sky. They bring mariners off rough deep water, make

the night friendly for those lost in the night woods, and they

drive out the darkness

in every dark corner of every

dark house. The children

come in all colors, the children

come in he, she, and they. The children live in all countries, and they look

like everyone else—except for their hands, which always contain

the hands of others, so they can show us the way, pull us

right up off our feet, no matter how hard we

resist, like we always had wings, like we

always lived on higher ground in the starry, starry night.

SPRING ALONG THE SHENANDOAH, 1863

"Beat! beat! drums!—blow! bugles! blow!
Make no parley—stop for no expostulation,
Mind not the timid—mind not the weeper or prayer,
Mind not the old man beseeching the young man,
Let not the child's voice be heard, nor the mother's entreaties…"

Walt Whitman

Fried chicken, collards, and biscuits were cooking up
in the kitchen, and I could hear my Aunt
Martha tell a story about how, when I was five, I climbed
a cherry tree and sat down on an entire house of red ants.

"We slipped that boy into a warm dish tub for an hour
and rubbed comfrey and goose grease into his little raw
fuzzy behind. The whole while

                    he was all grin and cherry pie."

A roar of laughter. Somebody smacked the plank table so hard
silverware went jumping clear to the floor.

"And that's why I brought a cherry pie to this wake today."

My little red-haired cousin peered around the parlor
doorway and looked in at me, but already
the rules had changed: I was in my body
in the box on the table, but I was also in the air.
I could pass right through the wall. I could see
everybody—my silver-haired father in his white
linen shirt; our neighbors, Mr. and Mrs. Birdsey; and my

mother, leaning back in her chair, still laughing, eyes
closed, hand over her face.

My younger brother drifted in, sat down beside the open
coffin, shaking his head at the bullet holes torn into my grey
uniform. But I must admit, if anyone just focused
on my face, I did look like I was asleep.

Outside the window, new green grass was coming
on the fields, and in the distance, I could see our cows
making their way down to the river. Hardwoods
leafing out.
                           Around then, I started to make
my way, too.

           "Goodbye, goodbye," I tried to say.

My brother scraping his feet back to the kitchen. My father
staring down at his big piece of cherry pie on a blue china plate.

LOOKING FOR AN ANGEL—FRIDAY NIGHT

"You road I enter upon and look around, I believe you are not all that is here,
I believe that much unseen is also here."

Walt Whitman

So many beats of the heart. So many roads to ride.
In the winter evening hours a man joins the mad
scramble out of town—the swirl of red and green
lights rolling in the early dark—and drives by
the little blue ranch house he's passed a thousand
times. The only difference is tonight
he pulls into the drive. The slippery
slate walk, the ill-fitting aluminum storm
door, the broken light switch in the foyer—tonight
he makes his way past all of it. He almost feels
at home after a vaguely familiar woman
appears out of a dimly lit room, throws her
arms around him and says, "You've
made it." And "Yes," he says. "Yes, I've
made it." Mutual embrace. Slippers. Mandatory
favorite drink. News. And while dinner's
frying up, he takes a good look at her
smiling over the onions—and that's what he
remembers as he drifts back over the slate
walk, and then the wheel in his hands, the steady
rumble of the truck's engine as he pulls
away, the shrinking blue light of the TV, and his
own foggy breath on the windshield. So many

heartbeats, he thinks. So many heartbeats along

a road filled with miles, disappearing crescent
moons and stars. And now, the tumble-down
farm house he passes every day, and tonight
he pulls in. Tonight when he pulls in, four
wagging-tailed Collie-dogs run to meet him, the hired
hand appears and relates a significant, but not
serious, barn problem as the man stiffly
dismounts from his truck—the porch lights
reflecting off the black arms of the maples, rail
fence, five little smiling blonde kids
appear in the windows—their squealing and laughter
intensifying as the man approaches a back porch
full of tiny boots, plastic sleds, last year's
bird's nest. And so many heartbeats, he thinks. So

many lives. This is what he thinks as he gets
back into the truck inside the reflected canopied
light of the maple trees. This is what he thinks as he
pulls back on the road, watching the five heads
disappear in the shiny yellow windows, and this is
what he thinks as he drives into the darkness, looking
for some clue to himself in every front yard—maybe
his vintage motorcycle, calico cat, the distinctive
color choice of his clapboard siding, or a face
he might recognize in a lighted doorway. Is
that the little girl I hold on my lap? Is that
the woman I speak to at night in a whisper? But the road
keeps going forever outward, and the man keeps
looking into the darkness as if somewhere
there's going to be a road sign or a mail box with his

name on it, but tonight there are no road signs, no
names on the mailboxes, not even a calico
cat, and as darkness envelopes the black
road, the truck, the vibrating wheel in his
hands, the man listens to his own heart beat
playing in time with the rhythm of his gigantic
Canadian-made V-8, thinking: Oh Man, the lives
we lead. Thinking that if he just keeps rolling
some good-hearted winged messenger will come out of
nowhere with a trumpet blast and say, with wild
gesticulation at every point of the compass, "Over
here, Stupid. Right this way. This is your life."

LLOYD WAXES HYPOTHETICAL
ON THE RAMPARTS OF NEW JERSEY

"I and mine do not convince by arguments, similes, rhymes;
We convince by our presence."

Walt Whitman

Let's say we're not pigs in grease. Let's say
the hour never came around—no old man
beating the shit out of me—no old

lady puking in the sink. Or let's say
it never got so hot candy melted
in the machines, or my best girl never

pulled the jam out of two guys for
a laugh, her panties wound tight around
her knees. Or maybe I never pulled
a limelight cruise doing ninety in a coal
black Ford like Sonny-Never-Die—
like I never was some sweet lover wolf-boy.

Let's say the hour never came down.
Or let's just say, you better watch my teeth.

A TEACHABLE MOMENT

For Brendan .

Over four years later, I'm taking apart my office in the library—which really isn't an office if we're being honest. It's more like a Beat shine to higher education, a bohemian expressionistic art gallery, and a clandestine, highly illegal kennel for black and white therapy sheep dogs all rolled into one. But the dean wants me to move to the new building, and being a sensitive man, I do. I take down the piñata; the two five foot Greenland kayak models suspended from the ceiling; box-up the ancient Royal Gotham City Press typewriter; roll-up the treasured Jack Kerouac grave stone rubbing—and then I see it: the ripped piece of paper with your name and cellphone number stuck to the wall. "If you need me, I'm there," you wrote. So I do the obvious thing: I call the number and leave a message in the inside-of-a-seashell silence that follows.

"I need to speak with you one more time. Can you stop by?"

A couple of hours later, when the light starts going down, I can almost imagine the door swinging open, and there you are with Clarence the Pit Bull and your brand new spectacular electric blue and white Nike Air Max, crisp jeans, Paul Pierce Boston Celtics jersey. I nod towards the over-stuffed purple chair on wheels, and you sit down with your ear-to-ear grin. From my angle, you almost look the same. Clarence jumps into your lap. He looks like the dog on the old RCA Victor records, and if I try hard enough, you look like nothing more than a boy and his dog, but your smile reminds me of the first story you told me when you were a freshman.

"I was twelve, kicked out of my house, living on the street, and a Jamaican family picked me up. A month later, I was living in their closet with my own thirty-five thousand dollars in a shoe box. There are some things they don't know how to teach you in college."

"I'm going to start from the top," I hear myself say. "And I don't want to be interrupted this time. Understand."

I imagine your smile growing a little wider—as if something like that's possible. You lean back in the chair, stretch out your long brand new jeans in front of you and cross your legs at the ankles.

"OK with me, Boss. You talk and I listen."

Clarence jumps down, does a half circle, and curls into the rug with his nose to your feet.

I watch you close your eyes once, look back at me and nod. I turn in my chair and look out the window for the thousandth time and focus on the Juniper green islands in the middle of the lake—and take it from the top.

"OK, I'm sixty years old, I go to my sister's Halloween party, and my three-year-old niece comes running up, jumps in my lap, and does this thing where she stares into my eyes from an inch away. I mean intense bottom-of-the-well kind of staring."

"She a little ass-kicker?"

"She's spawn from an entire family of crack-pot revolutionary ass-kickers. Centuries of them. Anyway, she's staring into my eyes, and all of a sudden, she takes her pointer finger and pokes the middle of my left eyebrow, hard—and I see stars. She pokes this old BB-size scar that nobody can see in the middle of my left eyebrow. I mean, I almost topple over, it hurts so much, and she says, 'What's dat, Uncle Jim? Did you always have dat?'

"I sew myself back together, and I tell her, 'No, darling. I got that when I was a blacksmith.'"

You jump in. "Oh, right, right. I remember this part. Now, how did you become a blacksmith?" High school play rise in inflection.

I turn back, look at Clarence, who looks like a black and white inner tube, and then up at you—until your face explodes in laughter.

"You know, I was hoping for a receptive, respectful audience this time."

"I'm here to listen," and the smile fades from your face, but not your eyes.

I go on.

"OK. I tell a lot of stories to my students, as you know—it's the way we roll in class, but I've never told this one, nobody has ever heard it, I mean, nobody, but I'm telling it to you."

I glance over. You're sitting there with your eyes closed, and I watch you nod. Now, there's no getting out of it.

"OK, I'm twenty-three years old, had a face like a puppy's belly. I was in graduate school at Penn State in Comparative Literature, and it wasn't clicking."

"What do you mean?"

"Wasn't clicking with the director of the program. If you told her not to cry over spilled milk, she'd start looking for the wet spot on the kitchen floor."

"Know what you're saying."

"Not long after came the coup de grâce."

"What's that?"

"Let's just call it an academic mercy killing. I'm supposed to be in the library reading Plutarch—who I am finding extraordinarily uninteresting—and somehow, I get my hands on a Peter the Great biography. I mean, the man was rocket fuel: he thought a person was uneducated unless they knew how to work with their hands. So Peter studies with master shipwrights, carpenters, stone masons, you name it. And I was gone. Quit school. My hair was on fire. Six months later, I had graduated valedictorian of my blacksmithing class. I mean, I actually had a diploma, a black dog, an ancient black Ford truck with a smoke stack coming out the back cap. I was running around these Green Mountains, working so hard, tools would drop out of my hands at the end of the day. Really, playing music in a little band, had a girlfriend, making money."

You lean back in the chair and stretch out your legs a little.

"Nice. Everything's OK when you're getting laid."

"Then I got this call from a young woman. 'Our place is too complicated to explain directions. Meet me at the Robert Frost pull-off above Ripton at 6:00. We got us a few cow ponies and we got us a couple of mules,' she said, 'and they need your help. Yes, sir.' I remember repeating that phrase after I hung up the phone. 'We got us a couple of mules, we got us a couple of mules. Yes, sir, yes, sir, yes, sir.' Sounded like a song, but if I had had any sense, I would have started running for cover right then.

"I had Babe, this pretty little black collie who would go everywhere with me—and she had the smarts, too. Could round up horses, just about read people's minds, and that's what we were back then: black truck, black dog, blacksmith. It was a go-team-go sort of situation."

"Same here," and you reach down and give Clarence a rub in back of his ears.

"We get up to Ripton about fifteen minutes early, break of day. That was our agreement. 'This here job's going to take the whole-dang day,' she said. There's plenty of light, but the sun hasn't made its way over the mountains yet and everything you look at is jaw-dropping beautiful. It's the end of August, and we were having a string of days close to ninety, but the color's starting to come down from the higher elevations. There's a thrown-up road up there that goes to the old Nobel Farm, and Robert Frost had himself a cabin above the farm—a hide-out is my guess. From up towards the Frost place in the silence, all of a sudden a lark pipes up, and it's the most beautiful thing. 'The air just tart enough,' Walt Whitman said. My Black Babe hears it and leans against my leg, and for a moment, I don't think it could get any better. We stayed like that for a good ten minutes. Sometimes, almost forty years later, I can still feel her leaning against my legs. She was one sweet black collie. She could round-up horses for me, just about read my mind. Never be another like her."

"That's what you said."

"We were frozen like that until we heard the grinding of gears, and then that sound when a truck uses its transmission to slow down on a hill, that hard whining. Next thing I know, there's a jeep truck bouncing in off the forest road, and let me tell you, she was a beauty. Logger's winch on the front bumper, eighteen inch tires. Forest green on the top side with deep brown running boards. Didn't realize it until later, but the paint was flat and not one piece of chrome. It looked like the forest with a steering wheel. Couldn't take my eyes off it until I saw the driver."

"All right. Now, we're getting somewhere. Keep your truck, Jim. I want to hear about how that Frost cabin had a double bed. Now, you're telling a story."

"You're not going to hear about that, but I will say, hippie girls back then did have their own version of style, and it was pretty easy for my twenty-three-year-old self to take it all in."

"I'm listening."

"The truck stops, and here's this girl with a huge furry Stetson and a halfway grin. 'Are you the man that's going to shoe our mules?' She tilts her head and she flashes me a smile that, for a second, reminds me of a cartoon wolf. Maybe it was the way her tongue rolled on her teeth. I don't know. I know Black Babe saw it, too. I felt her shrink just a little. When I nod yes, that girl runs up, jumps into my arms and kisses me on the cheek."

"Sounds like a good start."

"I don't think she could have looked any more like Annie Oakley. Her face was in the thirties somewhere, but that little body of hers was still eighteen. Maybe she was five foot one; had on some short little suede culottes with a feather fringe that just about touched her knees; a tight little suede leather vest over a green western shirt with yellow polka dots—the kind of shirt with snap buttons—leather gloves with a short fringe on the cuffs; jet black cowboy boots with tooled silver on the toes; long brunette cowgirl braids under that dark brown beaver Stetson."

"I don't care what she's wearing. What's under the clothes?"

"Well, we can start with her hug. It's was long and tight. When she finally let's go, she pushes off a little, like all of a sudden I'm in her way.

"'Howdy, I'm Prairie Rose.' Mighty handshake. Home on the Range. If there was ever a more perfect name for someone, I hadn't heard it. I also have to say that I noticed her polka dot shirt was left unsnapped two buttons more than I was used to. I couldn't help but notice that she had on this blue bandana halter arrangement on the inside, and I'm sorry I'm telling you I noticed, but I did, and she saw me notice and flashed me a halfway smile that if I had any sense I would have jumped back in my truck with my black dog, peeled rubber, and not looked back until I had crossed into the next state, or Canada, or someplace where whoever or whatever is following you, gives up at the border.

"Nothing wrong with that. Girl just wants to get bagged."

"If 'getting bagged' is what I think it is, that was not on her agenda."

"Obviously, she needed a more refined, sophisticated gentleman with a pit bull."

I imagine you lean in your chair, throw your head back laughing.

"'All you're going to need is your shoeing box,' she says. 'We got us everything else imaginable back at the ranch.'

"I mean, she actually said 'back at the ranch.' That's right. 'Back at the ranch.'

"She gives me a short, definitive nod that was accentuated by the Stetson, which I thought was pretty cute. When I think about it now, I think about those Zane Grey movies of the 30s. Prairie Rose was playing the girl who grew up riding bare back, chewing on saddle leather and sweet feed—where the deer and antelope play. I wasn't quite sure yet what part I was playing, but for those first few minutes, there were no discouraging words, not a cloud in the sky. I grabbed some extra nails, made sure I had a brand new fresh rasp, and a small stainless dish for Babe. I never liked to see my girl get dehydrated on the job."

"Always hydrate your dog, Jim."

"Prairie Rose's jeep truck was a real wonder—my dream truck. The bed was rigged to dump, and it had a mighty front bumper cable winch, and a beautiful hand-made back bumper with an assorted ball hitch arrangement. Both were painted flat black. For that matter, the entire truck was painted in flat paint, forest green with brown fenders and running boards."

"You've already told me that, and I've already told you—enough about the truck."

"I did? The running boards weren't original but home-grown out of thick boilerplate. Somebody had a real vision with that truck and stuck with it. The cab was just as good. Fire extinguisher, two magnetic army-issue flashlights, spotter's scope, and there was a vintage Winchester lever action .30-30, with the rare pop-up rear sight—hooked to the roof. She saw me look at it. 'That there's for snakes.'"

You shake your head vigorously from side to side.

"My ass. Don't think so, Jim. Don't you know people carry guns to kill things? Things like you? Who's that little lord you were telling us about in class?"

"Little Lord Fauntleroy?"

"That's him. This girl's already got you pegged as the Little Lord."

I hold that idea, and then go on.

"So, I watch her face fall for a second or two, and then come back on. Babe and I jump in, Prairie Rose giving me one of those where-the-buffalo-roam smiles. 'Now, Buckaroo Jim, you better hold on tight and strap-up because this-here horse likes to run.' And she wasn't kidding."

"Buckaroo?"

"That's right. You'd have been Buckaroo Brendan. And that girl could drive. The whole time—and I'm talking well over a good hour now, maybe more—she's talking to that truck like she was riding a horse, urging it over a steep incline, urging the truck to focus going over a little creek. 'Careful, Maude. Step lightly now. Onward, onward, that's my girl,' brush slapping at the fenders, tires throwing dirt and gravel. 'Buckaroo Jim, you best pull them mirrors flush.'"

You look at me with that signature full-face grin.

"If you aren't going to visit that double bed at the Frost cabin, I'm losing interest."

"We're not going there. Now, the first twenty minutes or so was old growth, deep woods, older oaks, maples, and beech. But then the road started to climb dramatically, and I watch Prairie Rose almost sit up in her seat, like she was getting off the withers of that machine. At the top of the rise, we burst through into an old clear-cut. Looking back down into the valley, the sun was steaming off the early morning fog. We crossed water three or four times, and she could rev that truck up any teeth-jarring climb, and then inch her down into gullies that were cool and dark. We get to a place where the road crosses a good-size brook, and she pulls up. In the course of her driving, I did happen to notice that those culottes of hers were riding high, the feather trim a good three inches above her knees."

"OK, I'm listening. Finally. Now, that truck's got a bed, too."

"She reaches down under her seat and pulls out this beautiful vintage collapsible feed/water bag the cavalry used to feed horses on the march. I had seen one at the US cavalry museum at Fort Robinson when I was a kid—but this one looked brand new. Prairie Rose turns to me and puts her hand on my knee. 'Now, Buckaroo Jim. I have something sensitive to ask you.' She is leaning in a little towards me and Babe, and I honestly wish I could say I didn't notice, but during all that hard driving, another snap on her shirt had let loose."

"Praise God, Almighty," you say, "let this be the beginning of something."

"Sorry. 'Now, Buckaroo Jim, the rest of the way to our place has to remain a secret. Would you mind putting this on? It will be better for everybody if you don't see where you're going.'"

"Are you serious? She asked you to put a bag over your head?"

"That's right. When I think about it now, it wouldn't have been much to start walking back to the town road—maybe a couple of hours. Black Babe would have loved the walk, I could have gotten in my truck, gone back home, maybe even shoed a few horses, made some money, checked in on my girlfriend. And don't think I didn't know what was going on: clearly these people were growing contraband up there in the middle of nowhere, and I clearly didn't have to be a part of it, but I didn't do that. I gave her a little smile, and pulled that canvas feed bucket over my head like it was an over-large top hat, and I was on my way to the junior prom. For her part, Prairie Rose was giggling and laughing the entire time."

You look at me, put both hands over your face, start rubbing your eyes and shaking your head.

"This isn't good, Jim. You let her put a feed bag over your head?"

"That's right. I let her put a feed bag over my head, and when she ties a little bale string around my neck to secure it, Black Babe growls at her."

"At least the dog has some sense."

"'Yes, sir,' she says. 'This here's a rider. Now, don't you look a sight?' The inside of the sack smells like dried apples and sweet feed, and after she cinches that string around my neck, she gives me a little squeeze on the elbow.

'Breathing OK?' she asks me, barely able to contain her laughter. I feel Babe dig a little deeper into my chest. 'Sure thing,' I say. 'Let's go.'"

You shake your head and look at the ceiling.

"This isn't good, Jim."

"Maybe. I do have to say, Prairie Rose was one hell of a conversationalist, a nonstop barrage of questions about my entire story— where I was from, where I took up the trade, how long I've been at it. At one point I felt like I was getting interviewed, and now, over forty years later, I think I was.

"'Done much corrective shoeing, Buckaroo Jim?'

"I tell her about how much of a challenge it was, and how, every once in a while, everything comes together, and instead of walking, a horse could just float over the ground.

"Minutes later, we were roaring up the mountain again, shivering dog in my arms, Prairie Rose sweet talking that truck.

"'Easy Maude. Easy Maudie. That's my girl.' We stop a little while later. I hear Prairie Rose laugh, and I hear someone getting into the back.

"'Yes, sir. Now, you hold on tight.'

"She grabs my hand and puts it around a handle attached to the truck's roof. At first the truck skids, then grabs, and then, like magic, the back end follows. We're going up something forty-five degrees, but the engine's running at just over idle. It's insane, and she's right next to me, giggling, 'Yes, sir, yes, sir, yes, sir.'

"Once or twice I was certain we were going to roll, but that Jeep truck always righted. We did about twenty minutes of this, then landed on the flat, and after going back and forth for a few minutes, rolled on the smoothest road I had ever been on. Felt like we were on a cloud.

"Even with the feed sack on, it was obvious we were in the bright sun. Then, abruptly, everything went black, and the air was cool and dank. We roll through deep darkness for over a minute—the whole time Prairie Rose asking me what kind of life I wanted for myself.

"'I want to sign up for that Bob Dylan song: 'Build me a cabin in Utah, marry me a wife, eat rainbow trout.'

"She grabs my knee when I said it. She grabs my knee and gives it a good squeeze. I didn't tell her to cut it out."

"Did you say, 'A little higher, darling, and a little to the right?' I'd offer her a second stick shift right about now."

I imagine your face exploding in the shadows, head going from side to side.

"You would. When we pour out into the light, the road gets bumpy again, and after we come to a stop, someone pops the hood, and we sit there with the engine running.

"'Buckaroo Jim, what kind of horses you want to work before you die?'

"'Mules,' I said.

"She laughs hard, and then somebody else's. A man's laugh.

"'Boy, I knowed you were the one the first time I laid eyes on you. Yes, sir. Ain't that right,' she says, like she was expecting someone to agree.

"We take off again, this time over what felt like a plain old dirt road. Ten minutes later, the truck stopped, and Babe lets out a soft low growl.

"Someone, very gently, unties the bale string around my neck and lifts off the feed bag. And I'm there blinking."

I imagine you throwing up your hands, asking me to stop.

"OK, let me guess. There's a big dude there and he's got guns."

"Well, yeah. There is. 'Buckaroo Jim,' she says, 'welcome to Hole in the Wall Ranch. This here's Big Country, the man who's going to give me my babies.'

"Whoever it was who named Big Country did so very appropriately. He was a good six-foot-six, six-foot-seven, and went about two-fifty, I'd guess. Besides that, he had an immense mane of strawberry blonde hair that dropped over his shoulders on his green western shirt. That guy was wearing black wooly chaps and vintage snake skin boots.

"I have to say, at twenty-three years old, I didn't know people like this existed. I mean, I was in the movies that I grew up watching. *High Noon, Lonely Are the Brave, Hondo, Pale Rider.* It was cool.

"His smile got a little broader as he stuck out his hand, but I have to say, shaking his hand was like shaking a catcher's mitt. Sure enough, Big Country was one impressive man, but it was the Van Dyke that put him over the edge. Full frontal, the guy looked exactly like Buffalo Bill— perfectly waxed handlebar with a sculpted chin beard that was a couple of shades redder that his face.

"All the dark colors in Big Country's outfit made a startling contrast to the two pearl handled revolvers that he wore crosswise. They almost looked like they were suspended in mid-air."

You sit there shaking your head.

"Now, Little Lord Fauntleroy, am I supposed to be surprised that he was armed and wearing five-hundred dollar boots?"

"Just listen. 'Welcome to Hole in the Wall, Buckaroo Jim,' and I stood there shaking his catcher's mitt. Now, mind you, this guy did not go to the Andrew Carnegie school of handshaking. He didn't shake like it was the last thing he was going to do on earth and then go to sleep for the rest of his life. Oh no, he shook your hand like he was holding a lost day-old blind kitten.

"'Yeah, boy. Big Country's going to fill me full of babies, and we're going to have us a mess of little buckaroos around here—and then out there in Wyoming, ain't we Country?'"

I can see your over-wide smile.

"Now, she didn't need Big Country to do that for her. She could have relied on Buckaroo Brendan. My pistol shoots bullets, and I got plenty of lead."

I pause, do that teacher thing, tilt down my head a little, and run my hands over my forehead like I'm getting a headache.

"Just let me tell the story."

"Go ahead, Jim. Sorry."

"So Country looks down at her with his mile-long smile, and she looks up at him with her sweet grin, one arm slipped around the small—if that was something you could even say—of his back, her head burrowed into the left side of his chest.

"'Yes, ma'am. We sure as hell are. A big mess of buckaroos.'

"They stand together like that for a moment until she busts loose and starts running down the road."

"'Follow me, boys. We got us some work to do.'

"Now, there's one thing you have to understand about 1977 and hippies. You could have a serious mental illness and could fit right in.

Dress any way you wanted. I mean, you could go to school dressed as a sixteenth century samurai, and nobody would say a word, except maybe, 'cool.' Everything was OK. So this western thing these people had going, I didn't even blink.

"After having my eyes open for a few minutes on this mountain top farmstead, I couldn't help but think these people were stuck in 1880, time traveling. Maybe their life was all theater. I just couldn't help but wonder what part I was playing—the blacksmith with his black dog, I guess.

"Black Babe followed me down the road with her tail and head down. Every once in a while I had to turn around and coax her to keep up."

You cross your arms in front of your chest.

"I agree with the dog. This pair is already creeping me out. Good thing you have me in your life to protect you. How did you ever make it this far?"

We stare at each other for a second or two before I go on.

"The log barn Big Country walked me into was truly a work of art. The logs were all dove-tailed, meticulously debarked and smooth. Immaculate, well-oiled harnesses are hanging from the wall with vintage pitch forks, carved wooden handled shovels, a fine tree-branch handled axe that is just gleaming silver. All my life I had wanted to visit a ranch museum, and now I have just walked into one. On the south end, they have two huge windows covered with a grid of ornately twisted metal bars for protection. The entire barn is bathed in sunlight, and there's a thick plank floor and two sets of beautiful cross ties.

"Three feet over your head, they have a chandelier of gas lamps hanging from a crossbeam. Any time, day or night, that place is ready to work.

"Big Country puts his fingers to his lips and let out a shrill whistle—one long, two short, and from a distance, I could hear a low thunder.

"A minute later, a bunch of mustang cow ponies come galloping

106

across the field. All of them seems to wait in line at the fence to say hello to Prairie Rose, who's got her horse voice going on. That girl vaults over the fence and sets down lightly in the middle of those mares, and they're all noses and nickering. Then she jumps on one backwards—laughing, and lays right down on her back as that mare starts to trot around the paddock. The entire time I watch her, you couldn't have slipped a piece of paper between that girl and that horse's back. Prairie Rose spins around and starts to lope in a circle, the other six in a line in back of her. Next thing I know, she's standing on that horse's back, arms out straight, like she's flying.

"Big Country looks at her and shakes his head. 'Buckaroo Jim, come on now. We can't watch this circus all day. We have to do us some work.'

"I follow him over to another small log barn, and inside, standing in straight stalls, were two of the prettiest black mules I had ever seen. Big Country hitches both leads and looked at me like I was supposed to tell him what to do next.

"'I need you to walk away from me, then towards me, do the same thing at a trot, and then do it all again at right angles.'

"Prairie Rose appears out of nowhere and grabs Ruthie, the jenny mule, who was ouchy on her front end. U-Haul, the jack mule, could walk just fine, but he had a center crack up front, an uneven gait and was forging—his back right was hitting his front right at a trot.

"I could see both of them needed to tell me more information, but they were first waiting for me to speak.

"I let them have the bad news, and start apologizing because I was going to have to make shoes. Prairie Rose's face gets big and Big Country smiles like the Rio Grande.

"'Buckaroo Jim, we're ready for you.'

"I follow both of them across the courtyard to another log building. Prairie Rose opens a sliding door, and inside was a complete blacksmith shop, coal forge with a hand-crank bellows, hardies, hammers, tongs. There's an immense two-hundred pound anvil strapped down to a chunk of polished oak log. Big Country gives me an over-dramatic nod."

I watch you wiggle in your chair.

"Why am I supposed to believe this?" you ask. "The whole thing's nuts. What about the drugs? And are you going to bag this girl or what?"

"You just sit right there and listen. Understand? I won't be long."

Clarence lets out a long baleful sigh.

"See," you say, "see what you're doing to my dog?"

"I'm getting there. OK. So Big Country turns to me and says, 'Already got the coal fire going for you. Prairie Rose, darling, would you please take Ruthie? We'll start on U-Haul.'

"Now, I'm going to tell you this next bit of information under the umbrella of Walt Whitman, who said, 'If you done it, it ain't bragging.'

"Regardless, I probably had my best day as a craftsman that afternoon, felt like someone else was doing the work with my hands. Pure magic.

"Big Country had some coiled automobile spring, and twenty minutes later I had made a header and pritchel punch. He also had the perfect horseshoe stock on hand that he salvaged from a spring-tooth harrow. I won't go into specifics, but U-Haul needed a rolled toe and beveled quarters for his center cracks. I made Ruthie bar shoes up front. I lapsed into that flow state you get when everything's going right. It was crazy—like someone else was doing the work with my hands lickety-hell for three hours. It's an ancient process, your fingers doing things that fingers have been doing for hundreds of years, like it's some memory deep in the bone just waiting to come out. Don't ask me, though; I can't explain it, I just know that you could have wrung out my clothes and collected five gallons of sweat and mule hair."

"My fingers know how to do a few things fingers have been doing for centuries, too." You chest heave in laughter and start admiring your hands. "Jim, your hands might be PG, but mine are rated R."

"But I'll tell you, those mules were two sweethearts, and when I was all done, Big Country trots Ruthie around the dooryard, looked at Prairie Rose and shrugged his shoulders. Neither of them speak to each other, but every so often they'd lock eyes and come close to smiling. Prairie Rose gives U-Haul a spin. Both of those mules just floated over the ground, striding out effortlessly. I feel like I am under water, maybe it was the heat, but when I come to the surface, Prairie Rose is staring at me with her huge toothy grin, and Big Country is shaking his head from side to side.

"'Buckaroo Jim,' he says, 'I feel like I was listening to music. Have time to trim our ponies?'"

"So I go through all seven like I'm changing partners at a Contra Dance. Big Country is handling them for me on one side of the paddock, and Prairie Rose is in charge of bringing them to us. She's loping around, lazily roping one after the other, and let me tell you, that girl was one phenom. She was riding bareback, no bridle, no problem, talking to them the whole time.

"'Now little Sassy Britches, you come to Momma...'

"I go through all seven, and I'm there shaking Big Country's hand with his day-old blind kitten grip, my black collie right at my feet. Next thing I know, I'm down hard on the ground getting pulled across the gravel. Had the wind knocked out of me. Scraped my elbows right through my shirt. That girl had *roped* me. Pulled me right down on the ground, and she's right up there on her horse laughing her ass off.

"Big Country pulls me up, and turns to her with a big smile on his face.

"'Now, darling, you hadn't ought've done that to Buckaroo Jim.'

"She's up there on that horse doubled over laughing, laughing so hard tears are streaming down her face.

"'Oh, I am so sorry, boys. It's just that roping…'

"She can't get it together to even talk, so like a real diplomat, the big man steps in.

"'You just have to forgive her. She done it to me, too. This here girl would rather rope than eat.'

"She moves her horse close to the fence and looks down at both of us. 'Hell no, Big Country, you know me better than that. I'd rather rope than…' And then slightly, almost imperceptively, she pushes her pelvis into that horse's withers a couple of times, throws her head back, then side to side, laughing.

"'Now, Big Country, if you ever bring in another man, this here's the one, but first you better cool this boy off or he's going to turn into a raisin right in front of us.'

"Country slowly averts his eyes and motions me to go over to his water trough. He has an antediluvian cast iron water pump painted up dark green and yellow that spills into a gorgeous wooden horse trough. That was the thing about the entire place. Every damn thing was gorgeous. It looked more like a movie set than a farm. I half expected someone to jump from around a corner in a black beret and holler: 'action, cut.'

"'Here, you put your head under there for a minute, and I'll change your mind.'

"Seconds later, I knew what he was saying. That water is ice cold, like melted snow, and whatever I had been thinking before was long gone.

"At this point, Prairie Rose comes over and is half whispering to the big man, who has to lean over about double to accommodate her. He straightens back up and looks at me a little sad-eyed.

"'Need to show you our corn, Buckaroo Jim.'

"About fifty yards down the hill from their barns and cabin, these guys have a long, beautiful corn piece that I'd guess is about five acres or so, stuff is way over your head, giant tassels, long ears, nice and round.

"We get to the edge, and Big Country hesitates for a moment, looks at Prairie Rose, who looks back and gives him one small nod. He turns and walks into the plot."

You look at me and just shake your head.

"If you walk into that corn patch, it's all over."

I look back and shrug my shoulders.

"Prairie Rose grabs my hand and pulls me towards her. 'Follow me, son.'

"She leads me in, Black Babe right behind me, for about fifteen rows or so, holds my hand tight and then squeezes it hard a couple of times.

"'Come on, slowpoke.'

"When I catch up with her, I can see a break in the light, and then I am sandwiched between them both, Country looming on my left, Prairie Rose letting go of my right hand. Stretching out in front of us is a field of pot ten feet high, as far as the eye can see."

"No shit. Do you have any idea what something like that's worth?"

"No idea. My first guess would be a lot. Regardless, the two of them are standing there like they've just discovered America.

"'This here represents our ranch in Wyoming, Buckaroo Jim. Big Country and I are very cordially inviting you to throw in with us.'"

I imagine you sitting up in your chair, leaning forward. You spit out the words.

"Even back then, that field would be worth a couple million— probably more. I can't even imagine what that field would be worth. How come you figure they asked you?"

"Horses."

"The people I've worked with were like family; that's all I can say."

I look back at the chair, feel a twist in my chest, and nod.

"Well, OK. Speaking of family, I need to say something about my mother right now, a woman who was filled with drop-dead observations about the world and the people around her. 'Jim Ellefson,' she said, 'everybody's human, but I have to say that you're a little more human than necessary.'

"Heartbreakingly true. I was dumbfounded looking at all that reefer, one mighty green ocean, immaculate, rows so long they got pointed at the end. And I'm standing there with the reincarnation of Buffalo Bill, who's wearing two pearl-handled revolvers on his hips, and a scantily clad Annie Oakley, who would rope and drag you down a hard road for a laugh until you had no hide. I can honestly say that I stood in the center of all that ganja, between those two strangers thinking they were my newest best friends."

"How much were they going to give you?"

"Ten times what I was getting shoeing horses and playing music. But you have to understand, it was 1977, and I was running on a Bob Dylan soundtrack. I was dancing to Taj Mahal. I wanted to live out deep in the country and 'paint my mailbox blue.'"

You wince, and put your hands over your ears.

"I don't know that music. I like Biggie and Jay Z."

"Anyway, after I say yes, Prairie Rose puts her arms around Big Country and says, 'Let's celebrate.' And he reaches somewhere in the back of his hat and pulls out a cigar-size joint. And let's be frank here: I was no church angel back then. Certainly, I had smoked my share of reefer, but this was an entirely different substance. The stuff was all bud, sticky, and smelled like it had all been sprayed by a skunk and then sprayed again. I take a big drag on that thing and let it out with a series of coughs. Prairie Rose thinks this is the funniest thing she has ever seen.

"'Looks like this here boy needs more practice.'

"The big man did his little sweet smile.

"'Yes, indeed, darling, but he sure is good with the mules.'

"Both of them have a good laugh over me, but for my part, I was disappearing into the landscape. The field had started to hum a little. I looked up at the tree line, and the maples looked like they had a pulse. One tree was dark green, and as I stared at it, it was slowly getting lighter and lighter. When it turned white, I fell on the ground to the tune of faraway Victrola laughter."

"So this guy knew how to grow some premium dope."

"Yeah, that's right, said he learned it all from the gooks in Nam. How to grow it, clean it, dry it. Even how to hide it. But I'm stoned on the ground, and I hear Big Country say, 'This boy needs to get wetted down.' Prairie Rose starts giggling and takes off.

"I get myself together enough to follow him cross the pasture and into the deep line of woods. Maybe it was the sound of the water coming down from the rock cliff above us, or maybe it was the image of Prairie Rose standing on the rocky edge next to her pile of clothes, laughing at us, just wearing the aforementioned blue bandana halter, but I stood there weightless, like any second I would start ascending into the heavens.

"'Will one of you boys please slip that knot in back? I cain't get it.'

"She looks right at me, raises her head and opens her eyes a little wider."

"She wouldn't have to ask me twice."

Clarence wakes up from your laugh, does a half circle, and then reforms his black and white inner tube.

I look back at you and laugh almost as loud.

"You think that's something everybody doesn't know? Your personal record as a rake is in the public domain, but for my part of it, if I could have teleported myself to Australia, I would have. I just kept looking back at the trail and tried to coax Black Babe closer to the rocks, so Big Country could do the honors.

"Seconds later, I hear her scream and hit the water.

"I had seen Maxfield Parrish paintings in college that had made me feel the same, but they contained those fragile nymph creatures. Not one of them could stand up on the back of a loping mustang, spread her arms airplane wide, and then act like she was shooting two six guns into the clouds.

"When Prairie Rose came to the surface, she swam over to a long flat rock that was on the far edge of the water, crawled out, laid right down on her back using a little rock ledge as a pillow and looked up at us with her hands in back of her head.

"There was a good thirty foot drop into the pool below.

"Big Country steps out of his boots, and seconds later his wool chaps, pants and shirt are piling up at his feet, but I did notice that his smile faded a little when he took off his guns. Black Babe and I had sat down and I was struggling to untie my boots, but in my peripheral vision, I saw him stare at me long and hard. His smile returned, and he carefully rested his pistols on top of his chaps, and then covered them up with his green snap shirt.

"'You boys going to be glad you dropped trou and jumped in,' she said.

"She sat right up, and in a flash, did a handstand on the edge of her rock, started to walk on her hands, and then flipped herself backwards into the water.

"'That there girl's crazy, wouldn't you say, Buckaroo Jim?'

"He had a leather lanyard around his neck that held a small

knife. He saw me notice it, shrugged, took it out, and rolled it back and forth through his fingers. It jumped from one hand to the other, like it was alive. Then, in a flash, he handed it to me. It was thin and light, beautiful bone handle, and it fit perfectly in my hand. The blade was so bright, it looked like there was a flame inside.

"'Now, careful. That sticker's sharp. I keep it that a-way. She's my last defense.'

"I laid the blade flat on my wrist, and very gently pulled back. It took the hair off—and a little skin. When I gave it back to him, there was blood on it.

"'Damn it, Shirley. Sorry, Buckaroo Jim. Shirley's always misbehaving. She seldom comes out of her sheath, and when she does, she's always causing trouble.'

"He wiped off the blood between his thumb and forefinger, and very delicately, put it back into the tooled leather sheath. Next thing I knew, he was flying through the air in a perfect swan dive.

"I jumped off feet-first a few minutes later. The drop was totally terrifying, but I stepped off the edge without any hesitation. Both of them were lying on their flat rock smiling and waving up at me. There was no use second-guessing.

"I stayed down deep in that pool for over a minute, and I came up panting with an ice-cream headache.

"It was exactly what I needed.

"When we got back to their cabin, the light was beginning to get a little rosy in that way late August sunsets do in Vermont, and all of it was flowing into the south side of their log cabin. I'm going to say cabin, because of the size. It was probably just sixteen by twenty, but it had a half story loft, skylights, and huge windows to the south, east and west. They had a restaurant-size gas range that Big Country had rigged up to use methane he made from chicken manure, right next to a Home Comfort wood range. Country had also built his own Finnish fireplace out of field stone.

"And somebody was an artist. There were oils, watercolors, and photographs everywhere signed 'RDC'—mostly of horses and western riders, but some were hunter jumper scenes, steeple chase, riding to hounds.

"I must have looked like a kid at the circus. This little house could have been another movie set, in the deep black hole of some time machine.

"Then I landed on a framed engagement announcement from *The New York Times* Sunday Styles section. The headline read: Olympic Riding Champion Rosemary Dulles Cabot to Wed Ensign and All-American Randall 'Big Country' Oxford. The photo next to it was a young, crewcut Big Country in a formal white Navy uniform, and Prairie Rose was dressed in the longest wedding dress I had ever seen. They were arm and arm, walking down the steps of a chapel under a canopy of raised crossed swords, held by eight uniformed young men.

"Everybody was beaming.

"Prairie Rose lit up when she saw me find the photo.

"'Yes, sir, that there's me and Country getting hitched at Annapolis right after he graduated. And all them boys became a part of his team. Now, all them boys live in heaven now, ain't that right?'

"'That's right, darling. All them boys live in heaven.'

"He said it slowly and carefully, but there was no western twang in his voice. He nodded when he finished his sentence, and I watched the smile come back to her face when she nodded back.

"'Wasn't long after that photo was taken that Country was deployed to Vietnam, and I didn't see him for nearly three years. They said he was MIA, presumed dead. That's when I got sick, ain't it? I lost our baby, and I had to go to the hospital. I prayed for Randall, and I painted them paintings for him, and I watched that movie *Butch Cassidy and the Sundance Kid,* over and over, and they got me that there book by Butch's sister, about how he wasn't killed in Bolivia and how he made it back, and that's when I knowed Big Country was coming for me. I dreamed he busted out of a cage, and I saw him teach them all a lesson.'

"Her body went slack.

"It's not that he ran across the room. Maybe the next thing to it, but he took her in his arms. She completely disappeared into the size of him, and he held her like that for a good five minutes, both of them silent, eyes closed, until she looked up and nodded.

"'Randy was a P.O.W. for a long while, and they had him in a bamboo tiger cage, didn't they?'

"'Yes, darling, they did, but I kept you close to me, and I never lost faith. Every day I said the Whitman poem to you. I stayed strong. I said it low to myself and to you.' He held her face in his huge hands and recited the poem.

"*I mind how once we lay such a transparent summer morning, How you settled your head athwart my hips and gently turn'd over upon me, And parted the shirt from my bosom-bone, and plunged your tongue to my bare-stript heart, And reach'd till you felt my beard, and reach'd till you held my feet.'*

"'Country made himself a bamboo knife. You taught them a lesson, and busted loose, didn't you? You taught them a lesson. You was one tiger too much for them, wasn't you? And you came back and busted me out of that hospital. And now, we're going to have us a ranch, and you're going to fill me up with babies, ain't you, Big Country?'

"'Yes, darling. You got that right.'

"He put his arms around her and held her again, and I watched her disappear into the great folds of his body, and I watched her little caved-in face start smiling again.

"When he turned back my way, he sent me a little wink and nod. When Prairie Rose spun around, her face went blank, fried egg eyed, and I swear she saw me for the first time.

"We all drove back in the golden light. The sun started to dip below the Adirondacks, and everything looked like a Monet painting all over again.

"Big Country said it was OK—I didn't need the grain bag over my head since we were partners. It wouldn't have made much difference. I don't think I would have found that place again if I unreeled surveyor's tape or dropped bread crumbs every foot. I had never seen such an elaborate route in my life. Their land was well off an abandoned railroad line, and all they had to do was run their truck up on the rails and deflate the tires a little. Big Country said it was standard operating procedure in the SEALs.

"'Everybody's staking out the roads or trails. Nobody thinks you're arriving by rail. Why, a few times we'd roll up right in the middle of a town, and just tap the locals on the back of their shoulders. Say howdy-do.'

"The dark stretch was actually a tunnel, and I helped Country air up the tires on the other side with one of those spark plug pumps, ease off the tracks onto a logging road.

"'That's it, Buckaroo Jim. You're already a pro, and it's just your first day.'

"We ran through the woods a good half hour or so, and then winched that truck down a forty-foot smooth cliff, nobody saying anything. I mean, we winched the truck, Prairie Rose at the wheel.

"On the way back, I sat back in the bed with Black Babe, and every once in a while Prairie Rose would glance back through the window. I'd give her a big smile and wave, but I didn't get one back.

"The rest of this story gets a little hard to tell, but I'm just going to say it. It was well past dark when we arrived back at my truck. Big Country loaded up my shoeing box. I was just about to get in when Prairie Rose walks up really close to me, that tongue of hers sliding across her teeth. It was the same wolf smile she had given me first thing.

"'Big Country, we made us a mistake. This here boy's a federal investigator, I reckon.'

"He just stood there still as a mountain, listening, closed his eyes for a moment, sighed, and looked at the ground.

"'I said he ain't the one, darling, and he's standing there laughing at us. He's going to turn us in, sure, if you don't do something about it.'

"He closed his eyes again for maybe five seconds. What came next is still wrapped up in a blur.

"He reached back over his shoulder, and his knife appeared in front of my face. I watched him roll it through his fingers, jumping hand to hand. It was like the knife, hand, and arm had turned into a snake. Then he stuck hard just above my left eye with the butt. He might as well had hit me with a ball-peen hammer. I immediately fell back into my truck, but he grabbed me by the shirt collar and gave me a shake, and I shook like Raggedy Anne.

"This part's hard to say, too, but I'm just going to say it. Blood was running down my face from the cut, but after the fireworks show in my head, I was just this sobbing thing at the end of his arm. There was nothing else I could do.

"Big Country was saying something to me, but I was still in the undertow. Then I felt her hands on my face.

"My good eye cleared for a moment, and I could see her smile and that long wolf tongue rolled across on her teeth.

"'Buckaroo Jim, we're trying to send you a message, but I still don't think you've quite got it.'

"I saw him blink just once, then his arm and hand swung low down towards Black Babe. A second later she was dead at my feet.

"Then he gave my collar another shake.

"'If you say anything about what happened today, anything about me or Prairie Rose, or Hole in the Wall, I'll kill you.'

"I felt myself nod, and then felt him release the hold on my collar. When he did, I slumped to the ground.

"Moments later, I heard their truck start up—and Prairie Rose's laugh.

"'Well look, boy, ain't you going to pay him? Buckaroo Jim did a right fine job on our mules and ponies, and it just ain't right to send him down the road empty.'

"I was still crying and bleeding so much I couldn't see, but I heard his footsteps on the gravel.

"'There now, Buckaroo Jim. I put some money on the floor of your truck. You done good. Thanks again.'

"He put his hand on my shoulder and gave it a little lost day-old blind kitten squeeze. When I finally managed to look up, I saw their taillights disappear into the darkness.

"It didn't take long for everything to unravel after that. Big Country had thrown in fifteen—no joke—hundred dollar bills onto the floor of my truck, plus a big bag of his killer pot, and believe me, I started to work on that right away.

"It turned out I had one hell of a concussion. Every time I walked outside, the light was so bright, I could only cover my eyes and stumble back in. I told the nurses in the emergency room that I had been kicked by a horse, and of course, everybody just shook their heads in sympathy at the lemon size bump on my eyebrow.

"I stopped answering the phone, too, and spent most of my time holed up in my house, staying up most of the night, walking around the floor like a ghost. Maybe I thought a jeep truck was going to appear in my dooryard, but more likely, I just didn't think.

"I had a good excuse for not going to work for a couple of weeks, and I ended up with one hell of a horseshoe shaped shiner that everybody oooed and ahhhhed about.

"I had made a lot of friends in that town, but it didn't take long for the phone to stop ringing, especially after the night my girlfriend's father stopped by. He gave me a long look, said he could smell reefer as soon as he opened his truck door.

"'It's time for you to try something else, somewhere else, son.'

"But I couldn't hear him. I couldn't even look at him. All I could see was that swinging arm of Big Country, and Black Babe dead at my feet.

"I never shoed any horses again, just treaded water for another six months, doing little handyman jobs, but then I did go. Everybody said I had lost my nerve, but that wasn't it: I had lost my heart.

"I got into graduate school out west, and I left that little Norman Rockwell town, drove my truck across the country, stopped in to see my grandmother on the way, and somewhere around then, maybe because of the book she gave me, I stopped feeling like a ghost.

"Almost forty years later, I'm a teacher and a writer now. I have a little book out with another one on the way; I spoke at graduation in my funny Renaissance academic hat, marched to the bag pipes; I shook hands with my students and even the president of our college, and I hugged parents, a lot of parents. At graduation, I smiled for over four hours without trying, and then on my way home, I thought about Prairie Rose and Big Country for the first time in years.

"I actually hoped that they had gotten away with it—that they sold that field of reefer for millions and were able to buy another Hole in the Wall Ranch in Wyoming. I hoped they had an entire herd of top-of-the-line mustang cow ponies, I hoped that U-Haul and Ruthie were still kicking, and I hoped that Prairie Rose had a bunch of little red-haired buckaroos, just like she wanted. And I also hoped that I had a few more years where my niece would poke her finger at the BB-size scar in my left eyebrow and ask me, "What's dat, Uncle Jim? Did you always have dat?"

I stare at your empty chair, and I imagine you ask the same question, but this time, I'm ready.

"So why are you telling me all this for?"

This time I don't say, "I don't know. No reason. I was just telling a story."

I swear I can almost see you, but the corners of this office have their shadows in your face. It doesn't matter anyway; the question is on the table.

"Why am I telling you this? Because I asked you to write about Mary Oliver's 'The Summer's Day' and I asked you the same question that she asks at the end of the poem: 'Tell me, what is it you plan to do with your one wild and precious life?'

"And I asked you to look right at it and not avert your eyes, but after you graduated with a degree in Professional Writing, someone offered you a twenty-five K job copy editing, and you worked that job for a couple of months, and then you moved in with your two old friends who sell weed, and you elevated the business, because you're business charming; you're a front porch dope dealer, honest weight, timely delivery, after-hours pick-up, financing available, extended credit for long time customers, bountiful choice of products. You say: "Please." You say: "Thank you." You smile when you don't have to.

"But you listen to me. You have to change your life, or this is what will happen.

"You'll take care of people for a couple of years, until there's a knock at the door. It's your best friend who is like family. This kid might as well be your younger brother—do you understand? He'll bring his pal, and after you shake hands, high five, and hug, you'll watch the Patriots take apart the Denver Broncos; you'll communally put away a giant, primo chicken parmesan dinner, and then, they will kill all of you. They'll slit your throats. They'll slice-up your dog, Clarence, and throw him in pieces on the bathroom floor. They'll take that eighty grand you kept in two shoes boxes in your bedroom closet, line you boys up like you're first graders at nap time, and sprinkle fine Afghani skunk weed all over your bodies.

"And this will happen, too. I'll watch your girlfriend melt down at your funeral, and I'll listen to your mother choke out a story I can't even understand, her face buried deep in my chest.

"Why am I telling you this?

"Years later, when I move my office, I'll find your cellphone number scrawled on a scrap of lined paper stuck to my bulletin board. The note reads: 'If you need me, I'm there.'

"So I go straight at it, in a teachable moment. I press in the numbers and when I hear the ocean on the other side, I say everything I need to say."

SELF-ACTUALIZATION ARRIVES IN THE NORTH COUNTRY

"This is what you shall do . . . and your very flesh shall be a great poem."
                                                    Walt Whitman

You need a maverick 87 degrees on May 5th with brook trout
rising out of the deep pools. You need a day off in the middle
of the week; a fearless black and white stock dog; antediluvian
side-by-side twenty-gauge upland bird gun; vintage Gibson
six string; fly rod; razor-sharp chain saw; immaculate, built-in
toolbox; front-end five-ton Tiger Shark winch on the Toyota
four-wheel drive.
                          And you need
a six-month-old hold-on-tight naked baby who likes to grab
you around your neck, girl or boy.
                          It doesn't matter.
                                             What you
don't need is your steel-toed logger boots, green buffalo plaid
flannel shirt, Carhartt double front work pants, and you don't
need to weigh-in on the concerns and opinions of the people
who drive by in their late model electric cars, or the Volvo
load of impertinent high school girls, somebody shouting, "Nice
ass, Gorilla Man."
                          Oh, no.
                                    Today, you and your baby need to
have your arms around each other, you need to wade belly
button deep across the sharp rocks and right into the middle
of the Jail Branch river, and you need to hold up your baby
at arm's length into the 87-degree May 5th sun, praise

the deep cuts on your frozen feet, the crystal swirl and sting of mountain snow run-off. Your arms around each

other, both of you holler, take a full immersion
dunk, spit it out and holler, holler, crack the sound
barrier—

        hear you all the way to the moons of Jupiter.

THE INGREDIENTS OF THE DAY

"The moon gives you light,
And the bugles and the drums give you music,
And my heart, O my soldiers, my veterans,
My heart gives you love."

Walt Whitman

I want to say the moon was hanging low like a white
sickle, Norman. I want to say I can still see it: moon like a white
sickle in the western morning sky, but I don't
remember the moon.

                       I do remember I was wearing brand new
shiny work boots, and I drove that day. I drove my mother's
Datsun 510 Sedan because your Roadrunner was getting its frame
straightened. We were listening to *Tommy,* the rock opera, dust
vibrating off the dashboard, fog rising straight up
out of the valleys. Norman, you were screaming into a microphone
fist, laughing Roger Daltry, hanging out the window, waving
to the cows, to anybody: *"See me, feel me, touch*
me, heal me"— left hand floating over your crotch.

I remember I was making $2.55 an hour, you close
to $4.00, and we had to dig fifteen holes for the Lessenger's
brand new entertainment addition, concrete coming
tomorrow, fifteen holes, four feet deep, three feet
wide in their rocky back yard, the bone yard, you called it. You
had worked on their pool and bath house. Mrs. Lessenger
was my mother's tennis friend, and Kerry Lessenger was the class
fox.

      By 10:00 we had four holes dug, it was 98°, Scotty

yelled "Fuck this," winged his shovel across the yard, splintering
the handle, roared away in his baby blue Camaro. Mrs.
Lessenger appeared, asked if everything was OK, served us
iced coffee and peach scones, clotted cream and sugar, asked me
if I really was going to declare Pre-Vet at the University
of Miami. "A party school, don't you think, Jimmy?" You
said you entered the University of Saigon in Pre-Vet three
years ago, but later shifted to agronomy and mortuary
science. "Study abroad can teach us so much about
ourselves," you added. Mrs. Lessenger asked if she could
serve us lunch later, and you declined, explaining you had
a job interview at the bank and had to run a short
errand at the post office.

                We dug. I told you if I dug another
foot, I was going to die. You said in Nam I'd die, or scoop
out the gravel with my bloody fingernails between
mortar rounds. "I saw some dumb shit get it for lack of a deep
hole, found the guy's lip, complete with whiskers, stuck
to the roof of my hooch forty yards away."

The sun rose over the roof and hung there so it could
sizzle the back yard, we dug three more holes, and on our
way to the car, Mrs. Lessenger asked if we would be so kind
to post four letters. "Glad to, Honey," you said, fifteen minutes later
as we sat down at Peachey's bar—two cheeseburgers, two
shots, a pitcher of beer. I paid. You ripped up the letters
and threw them on the floor. "I think that bitch
wants my ass, Jimmy."

                On the way back, I almost
swiped a dog off a corner, and you laughed, said I
should have squashed the fucker, said the first

person you killed in-country was an old lady Gook
with an AK47. "I want to pick up a couple
tabs," you said. "Stop at that red house."

I stopped. "What's a tab?" I asked, and fifteen minutes
later you came out wobbly with a girl with see-through
skin. "Who's that motherfucker, Norman Ellis," pointing
her shaky finger at me, and you looking
hard, squinty-eyed through the windshield

"He's nobody, Princess. I'll make him
disappear." And you snapped your fingers, pointed
down the street.
                    Norman, I remember I disappeared, stalling
once on the get-away, both of you falling over
laughing in the rearview mirror.
                              I almost took out the Lessenger's
mailbox, but got going again on the eighth hole. Around the tenth, Kerry
and two of her friends came out to take a "dip." They dipped
all afternoon, and I tried to focus on the dirt. "Come on in
when you get hot, Jimmy."
                          I waved and kept
digging. Mrs. Lessenger appeared sometime with an ice-
cold coke. I told her, as far as I was concerned, she
was the Coast Guard. She said she didn't understand. She said
she had already set me a place for dinner, had called
my mother, who did not need the car. "What happened
to Norman," she asked.
                        "Had a second
interview at the bank," I told her.
                                   "Well, won't that be grand."

I nodded, and spent the rest of the afternoon wondering
if there was a real difference between a girl's bikini
and a girl's underwear. Maybe color, I concluded.

When I finished, Mrs. Lessenger gave me some trunks
of her husband's that fit like a barrel, and I almost
lost them going off the diving board, came up, those
girls smiling too much.
                    We had chicken marinated
in orange juice, green beans, salad, blueberry
pie a la mode. Dr. Lessenger asked how I became
interested in Veterinary medicine. "James, there's
plenty of room in ear, nose, and throat."
                                        "It's my love
of animals, Sir. Ever since I was a boy." He nodded
like it was actually a good answer, and Kerry
walked me down to the car, said she really hoped
to see more of me.
                    "We'll be pouring concrete in the morning," I
told her, which we did, Norm. And somehow I had dug
an extra hole, a joke that lasted the rest
of the summer. You know how it is. Guys repeat.

We poured in the morning, and I remember the way
it worked: by lunch time, they had found you. Someone
had thrown you away. We heard you were all
needles and trash. Four feet down, three feet
wide in the rocky bone yard ground. Norman, I'm still
sorry. I never knew that last hole was going to be for you.

DEACON BILL'S SERMON CONCERNING WORK

"I hear America singing, the varied carols I hear,
Those of mechanics, each one singing his as it should be blithe
            and strong,
The carpenter singing his as he measures his plank or beam,
The mason singing his as he makes ready for work..."
                                    Walt Whitman

Work, Boys, is the man inside the man who wakes
every morning at 5:00 A.M. every
morning and starts his truck with a lunch
pail grinny grin and watches the light
rise off the green corn, wheels humming
sound track, wife's kiss still wet
on his son-of-a bitching lying

lips. Yes, Boys, God damn your souls
to Hell if work isn't the man who
looks his darling right into her strawberry
vanilla ice-cream face
                        and lies, says:
Peaches, I'd lie down and die for a minute
in your arms. Says: Peaches, I want to lay so
close, we breathe the same air. Says:
Little Darling, drop me in the ocean
I'd swim to the bank just to hear you call
my name so soft and sleepy. I'll say it

again, Boys, work is the man inside

the man who gets his darling breathing
hard while he's dreaming of buttering
bricks with fine lime mortar, or driving
ringed spikes deep into heart oak
—the ark of the swing electrifying his
hips, chest, arms, and fingers—electrifying
like Jesus, Boys

                    can you feel your hearts
rising around you, lintel, sill
and hearth, chimney box, rafters snug
to plates, purlins, razor straight
ridge cap.

                    Now, you sing it like it ain't
no church. Sing it like you know what your mother
made you to do. Sing it
loud enough so she'll hum along
from her grave in harmony. Yes
indeed, Boys, clap your frigging
Christly son-of-a-bitching hands.
Let's go and do us some work.

American Gothic

"O lands! all so dear to me—what you are,
(whatever it is,) I become part of that, whatever it is..."
                                                    Walt Whitman

There was only one drop of blood
at the signing, so imperceptively
small, even the lawyers, who were trained
to smell blood across a room, sat
oblivious.
                    The drop rose
out of the fingernail of his right
thumb, trailed down the pen, disappearing
into the ink. It was nothing, really, much
less than the sting of a bee.
                                        His wife
felt a mosquito bite, but an hour
later when the two youngsters walked
their very own fields, he could see
the damp red tracks following them
through the orchard grass.

For a moment, her eyes came off
his implacable face and took in the western sun.

It's all so beautiful, she told him.

He agreed, his hand
moving to the smooth neckline
of her black gingham dress. Dragonflies

circled fifty feet above their heads. Dragonflies
so thick you could climb your way
higher than the tree-top
ionosphere. You could rise
up. You could do a planetary
float until it's all
green, black, and blue.

You're so beautiful, he said.

They stood frozen just like
that until the light
went down into the evening
rising moon, into sweet crushed
hay, into sweet crushed hay
thick on their backs.

The next morning they started to find blood
everywhere: the cracked
steering wheel of his antediluvian
truck, the smooth hickory handle
of his splitting maul, her genealogically
acquired pie plates. Even a thin pink
patina floated on their prize-winning
French fingerling mashed potatoes.

Blood showed up particularly well on mail
from the town clerk, the state and federal
government. Blood even trickled
out of her three hundred thread count
Egyptian cotton sheets.

In fifty-three years they ran seven bloody
black dogs and kids while blood
oozed out of plane tickets for the family
life-changing trip to the Indian
sub-continent, art history
text books for the elite
metropolitan eastern college, certified
organic mesclun mix from the town
cooperative grocery.

They built their low-impact farmstead
off-grid on a high ledge of land, and built it
out of earth, straw, sand, and blood—a red
ochred garden wall, spring house, a magnificent
round utopian red barn.

Still, there were giant Cinderella
Pumpkins, bears in the berry
patches and garlic
the size of a fat man's fist.
                              Sometimes
he'd open his arms to all that milk and honey

I don't know if I'm half-full or half-
empty, he'd say with his abbreviated
grin.
        But he was way past half-empty.

She ran out of blood first and got carried
out of the kitchen, still in her lacy apron, past

an entire conflagration of square
sponge cakes, apple sauce, and bean salad.

He lasted another ten years, annually cutting
over ten cords of wood right up until every morning
he sounded like Rice Krispies, he sounded
like the metal on metal of bad brakes when he
walked across the wide pine floor.
                                    Instead of wasting
a good tool, they pried the pitch fork
out of his hard busted knuckled hands, and then
draped his blue work shirt and John
Deere hat over the tractor seat in holy
agricultural memoriam. A big
fried chicken and pork chop party, two
kegs, plus some very interesting new Australian
Beaujolais, twin fiddles, up-right bass, ancient
circle dances, bloody chest high hay
swinging in the late July evening breeze.

It's just the way it works.

Walt Whitman Breaks Out
(Of The Friday Afternoon American Literature Seminar)

For a moment the room bathed in golden sunlight. I stood
a little taller at the dais—my arms wide—and let the light
do its work on the white plumage of my head and tail.

Something, someone else was speaking words with my mouth
in the cinema of history: Pilgrims were making progress; Ben
Franklin was electrocuting himself flying a kite; Robert Edward
Lee rode Traveler through a grey sea of cheering
men; The Captain lay dead with a bullet in his brain; Chief
Joseph said he would fight no more
forever; and Admiral Dewey shouted, "Fire when you've
a mind to, Gridley."
                              And then the entire canon went off
at once: Emily began killing herself and everybody
else in Amherst, Massachusetts with Obsessive Repetitive
Rhythm Syndrome; Henry David tantrumed
from jail; from the crow's nest of the Pequod, Herman
spotted a giant white squid; Waldo stood at the pulpit convincing
us all that everything in the right light is beautiful; and Louisa May
introduced little women to little men.

                              Suddenly, I felt the maple floor
swell under my feet. "Ladies and Gentlemen," I said, "Take me
by the hand, and I will take you all
to The Good Place. Let me be your Sacajawea."
                              But with that, the guy
in the way-back who was sleeping all semester
tented under the roll-down map of America

groaned to his feet. In the six short weeks
of not seeing him, his hair and beard had turned ice-cream
white, and his loose linen shirt was unbuttoned
to his navel.

He spun around and shouted at the class: "This is what
we shall do: Love the earth and kids and dogs and everybody
else who's stupid and crazy. We'll give away our spare
change, and we shall hate these insulting, droning
tyrants and their copper-roofed soul-sucking brick
box snack bar schools—and we shall go out
freely amongst powerful uneducated people and mothers
and families and read out loud everyday in the biting
sun, rain and snow until the words get caught between
the line of our teeth, lips and lashes. We shall go—Oh
Hell, what are we doing here? Are you with me? Let's
just go out and write something."

After the initial roar
there was only the symphony of sliding chairs and drumming
feet. Jail break. Everybody jumping through windows. Everybody
busting down doors, not to mention, from considerably
down-hall, the unmistakable clank
of cavalry crossing a stream. A bugler sounded his horn.

In the distance, I could see flocks of what appeared to be naked
children cavorting over a fruited plain. I could see
a rocket's red glare. I could see broad stripes and bright stars
slowly rising over the great purple mountain American playground.

Walt Whitman Butts In Line
(At the Grand Central Oyster Bar)

I was just about to get seated when he
arrived. Evidentially, he was friendly
with the hostess, who kept repeating
Oh, My! Oh, Life! Oh, Walt this, and Oh
Walt that.
        It took him less
than a minute to float his big white mane
through the queue, and as he did, he stopped to kiss
everybody's husband, wife, kid brother, little orphan
girl auntie uncle boyfriend daughter.

I didn't even see him go by me until he was hugging
the hostess, his big hands stroking her amiable Iberian
behind. Her silver earrings gleamed under the lights.
        "How many today, *Tio?*"
"Maria, today, sadly, I am alone, *so*
sozinho," but then his furry face began to shine
as he looked straight up past the ceiling. He
laughed.
        "Once again, I contradict myself. Actually, I am multitudes."

And it was true. A mob appeared and pushed
past me to the front. There was a chubby Quaker, poling
raftsman, sailor rowdy, fancy-man and his Pawnee blood
brother, escaped prisoner, lunatic spinning girl, five striped-
shirted thieves, a hard-copy expunger, a camoed duckshooter
and twelve gauge, three blind sharp-hooved mice, wild gander
man, deaf but harmonious blacksmith, bloody butcher boy singing

"Greensleeves," fleet-footed slave, archetypal
trapper and his First Nation girl bride, Long Beach Island clam
digger, benevolent policeman, lobster-boy, ten enemies, sick
man with his doctor and his nurse, somebody's long lost
sweetheart, five suicides and their bloody knives, boys
and girls who love women and men, honest lawyer, a stallion
on his back feet rattling his chain, three old maids, and a couple
of smiling parents.

       The hostess looked at them all, grabbed some more
menus and shouted, "Oh, America! Oh, Life! *Que vida loca!* Follow me."

After the stampede, I was alone, except
for a train whistle in the distance. A conductor sang, "All
aboard for the Adirondack Zephyr: Yonkers, Croton-
Hamon, Hudson, Albany-Rensselaer, Saratoga Springs, White Hall, Port
Henry, Animosity, and Resentment."

       I heard some chugging down at the platform, quickly
retied my traveling shoes, and grabbed my old kit bag.

       Clearly, this was my ride, and it was time to go.

Under The Influence
(For my old teacher at Penn State, Jack McManis)

The more I keep trying to put Jack back together, the deeper and deeper he goes under dark water. Still, I can see him walking into the classroom with his white tweed coat and polo shirt, lips almost imperceptively moving. Almost. A few years later, he'd tell me that he recited "The Charge of the Light Brigade" to himself as he walked into every classroom, first day. Jack was one of those guys who wore his polo with the collar turned up in back—like a fin—inside the border of a V-neck tennis sweater. Pressed baggy khakis, and brand new ice cream white tennis shoes. At his desk, he'd wear his sport coat like a cape, over his shoulders and around his chair, and he always carried three or four books in his right hand, although when he wrote on the board, he could use either hand. He treated all of his books like they were the Bible or the Koran, and if you'd ever catch him walking between classes in the rain or snow, even under an umbrella, he'd have those books clutched close to his chest.

When I first saw him, I thought he looked like an exhausted, washed-out Robert Frost at the Kennedy inauguration, with a splash of Kerouac and Six Gallery. We'd all slowly learn later that Jack was a poster boy insomniac right out of Yeats, a bona fide "Wandering Angus" with a fire in his head, slept maybe five hours over three days, got sick a lot. Every change of season, he'd be down for a week or more. The man looked like a bull, but he could be knocked over in a light breeze. Most likely part of it was a compromised immune system from his early years of maniacal drinking, plus the fact that every large university might as well also serve as a gigantic petri dish. My no-good friends always kept after me about the reality of the student/teacher relationship. As they saw it, "Better get a recommendation out of McManis pronto, or you'll never get into Columbia. Once he's down there with the earth worms, forget it." Yes, we really were that self-absorbed, and I never did get into Columbia, devastating at the time, but one of the best things that ever happened to me.

Jack certainly had a style, but I was unsure of what style he was following, or maybe he had invented the hybrid Ivy-Beat. He had gotten into Columbia on the GI Bill, and Columbia "didn't quite know what to do with a hick from California." Regardless, the hick hit the curb and "took over the town for a few years. My town. My fair city. The Bowery, the Village, Harlem." Big shy smile, baby blues twinkling, no church angel. Apparently, Jack could dance, listen to music, and drink all night. White Horse Tavern, Birdland, The Blue Note, Kettle of Fish, The Cedar Tavern, Cotton Club. Said he was reborn at the Apollo Theater.

He was at the Cedar the night Jack Kerouac got thrown out for peeing in the sink. "As he was being escorted out the door, Kerouac shouted out that he was a writer, and someday everybody would be reading his stuff. The bouncer, a profoundly good man, said, 'Son, someday we all might be reading your stuff, but you're an asshole. Go pee somewhere else.' It was four or five years before *On the Road*, and Kerouac was already in a ditch. He should have called that book *Off the Road*." Class exploded in laughter.

Jack wrote a lot of good poems, and got published in some top places—*The Prairie Schooner, Poetry*—but never put a book together, never got famous. He was never driven to get his work out, but he was driven to write.

"You're welcome to fame, but writing's not about that." Writing for Jack was like brushing his teeth: it was an everyday thing, and if you didn't get around to it, you felt a little dirty, maybe even a little dead. For Jack, art was everywhere. "The miraculous appears every day, and you have to be ready to capture it." He wrote a poem about a maple seed helicoptering into his hand as he walked back from a class. He wrote a poem about passing an elementary school playground during a snow squall, and a little girl shouting up into the sky, "The angels are popping corn." He even wrote a few poems about his neighbor's ass, evidentially a miraculous thing in itself. When she went out to pull weeds on her side of the fence, Jack made sure the turf was well-groomed on his.

Jack appeared to be ancient, an oracle straight out of a poetry cave story book, and now years later when I do the math, I realize he was only fifty-five in 1972. I say only because, as I write this, I'm pushing sixty-three. Still, at fifty-five, Jack had bushy white hair, Disneyland snow white as his tennis shoes. Bushy, yes, but not bushy like some professors let their hair get in the early 70s. It was a well-groomed bushy—thick, and well-clipped around the ears on top of his road map face, a drinker's face, capillaries close to the skin, nose and cheeks tending towards red chopped hamburger, a small but noticeable scar along his hairline above his right eye. And although he wasn't a big man, five foot seven I'd guess, he had a brawler's shoulders and chest, and he had used them well on the tennis court.

When he came back from fighting in the Pacific in his crisp white uniform, he was nationally ranked, number five in the country, one of the many whose athletic career got interrupted by the war. He was Jack could-have-been-an-Olympian McManis, and I'd flash on what it must have been like, fleet-footed on the deck of a destroyer, trying to get depth charges into the water before the Japanese could unload a torpedo amidships, and if you happened to win the match, there was no jumping over the net for a handshake. "Whatever you do," one of my other professors told me with his huge black eye after catching a McManis serve in the face, "never play that little son-of-a-bitch in tennis. Sure. He seems nice, a real sweetheart, and he is in fact, but get a racket in his hand, and the guy turns savage. All animal."

And with it all, there was something almost shy—careful, small smile, looking out the window a lot as he spoke. No swagger, like some of my professors had. No, "It's show time, Ladies and Gentlemen. Let me be your Virgil. Let me be your Sacajawea." No circus. Introduction to Poetic Literature. I'm a sophomore at Penn State, and I was so happy to be there. In the 70s, you had to suffer for a year before you got the good stuff. It's September. I'm nineteen.

From the get-go, Jack made no secret of the fact that he was a retired drunk who flew the AA flag. Maybe he was a retired drunk and a half. He drank and took Seconal. He drank and took Benzedrine. The AA support and fellowship had saved him, and he put in a major piece of his life with his hand out to everybody else until he died. My own drinking wouldn't bloom out of control for another few years or so, but I was already working on it. I had the enthusiasm and the genes, the reverie, hooked from the first sip. Most of my relatives on both sides of my family were hard-wired. I was a monster in the making, and maybe Jack could spot it. I certainly can in my classes.

So many of Jack's stories started with: "I had been drinking for a few days…" or "I was drunk…" He told us once he had fallen down the stairs and cut his head open, a huge, nasty cut. "I don't know how long I lay in that pool of blood until my cat woke me. My cat kept pawing my face until I came to and got myself to the emergency room. That cat saved my life…" Or the time collegiate Jack woke up on a cold December sidewalk in Spanish Harlem. There was a black alley cat asleep on his chest—and Jack was without his pants. "The people in my neighborhood started calling me 'El Gato.' But the pants. Somebody had taken them, and my wallet, and my shoes. The cat followed me home, like a guardian angel. And I want to tell everyone in this classroom, that if you're stone drunk in Spanish Harlem at 4:00 in the morning walking home in the middle of December, primarily clad in your boxers, no one will give you a second glance, including the cops." Jack referred to his Lazarus-Narcissus self. He told us once, "If I had to say I was sorry to everyone I've hurt in my life when I was drunk or otherwise, I'd need a storefront along College Avenue and another lifetime. I'd call my place Jack's Redemption Center. I'd be open twenty-four hours a day in the apology business."

Right along with alcoholism ("once you're an alky you're always an alky") Jack had an intimate relationship with literature. New Criticism was going strong in 1972, and many of my professors just wanted to talk about the text: a scientific rendering of art systematically vivisected into its parts. All other information just got in the way of a close reading. For my part, I was interested in all the things that got in the way. I was there asking all the wrong questions. I liked referring to my own experience in essays. Not good. What about a writer's family and love life? Come on. What's Yeats without Maud Gonne? How much was Hemingway's war experience an impact on *The Old Man and the Sea*? What about: "But man is not made for defeat… A man can be destroyed but not defeated." Not relevant or important, I was told with a big smile, sometimes with a disgusted shake of the head.

And then there was Jack, telling us stories about writers, his favorites, like we're seeing them for the first time through a hole in the fence, the next stool in the bar. He even told us that Kerouac loved frankfurters and beans. No hot dogs, please. Frankfurters. And as Jack spoke, the greats began to populate the classroom; the greats began to populate our psyches. We were surrounded by LeRoi Jones and how he became Amiri Baraka. Elizabeth Bishop was drinking with Robert Lowell, who was not always the best of company. Jack said, "I saw the man turn on someone in the middle of a sentence." Edna St. Vincent Millay skipped classes at Vassar to write poems. "There she was, a poor hick genius from Maine on a full ride, and she calls Vassar 'a hell hole.'"

Pablo Neruda died of a broken heart in our classroom, and when Neruda read, he could fill a football stadium. People who didn't know how to read, would buy his books. People who could not read, would recite his poetry in Cantinas across Chile. Anna Akhmatova was a fearless voice in the snowy Stalinistic wilderness. Hart Crane said, "goodbye everybody," jumped off a boat in the middle of the Gulf of Mexico and fed himself to sharks. Sylvia Plath made her husband, Ted Hughes, look like a mental midget. Li Po drowned drunkenly trying to embrace the reflection of the full moon on the Yangtze River. On his famous American reading tours, Dylan Thomas stole clean shirts from his patrons and used alcohol to kill that thing in his brain that got in the way of his poetry, used to hang his coat on the blades of a circulating electric ceiling fan. Jack Kerouac liked cats and speed, and he loved speed because that way he could never stop drinking.

"Please don't try that," Jack added with a smile. "Not sustainable. Take my word for it."

And we did. Everyone in Jack's pantheon was made flesh with stories, but no one came close to the stories he told us about Walt.

Now, please take notice: It was never Walt Whitman. It was never Whitman. It was always Walt, and Walt was never a literary story book character. He never slipped into myth or sat on a throne, marble statue-esque. Walt became our crazy black sheep uncle, the guy we'd find sleeping under the dining room table on Christmas morning wearing Mickey Mouse shoes, the guy who had driven all night through a snow storm to be with us, car packed with presents, stockings full of Brazil nuts, licorice drops, wearing aftershave of one-hundred proof eggnog. After Jack was through with us, I felt like Walt was part of my family. I could smell Walt's breath when I walked around at night, which seems like what I did for most of my undergraduate education. Interestingly enough, I was never able to corroborate any of Jack's stories about Walt. Years later I would punch all the key words into Google and come up empty.

"Walt was thirty-five, went to bed one night, and in his dreams he had a revelation. In his dreams, he had been given a slice of how the world works. In the morning, his hair and beard had turned white—overnight— and he was totally and completely on fire. He was on fire for the rest of his life, and he lived to be an old man. For the rest of his life, he made it his job to give his epiphany to the rest of us."

"Walt would pace the streets of Washington D.C. or New York, followed by an entourage of homeless kids, garbage cats and dogs, every high and low-life of the city, everybody smiling, gesticulating, everybody laughing. Women with children. Old ladies. Old men. Walt had eyes like two fried eggs. He knew everybody, and everybody knew Walt. Walt was well-acquainted with Richard Wallach, the mayor of Washington during the Civil War. President Lincoln would smile and nod as they passed each other on different sides of Pennsylvania Avenue."

And then every once in a while, Jack would get us. He was a genius at finding that tender spot, and the next thing you knew, you were on fire.

"During Walt's life, he contributed his verse. Will you contribute yours?" he asked the class.

Jack would look out the window and smile, and I, of course, would look out the window and try to figure out what he was looking at. I never did, but I did realize after taking a number of courses with him that something outside that window would make him spring. Almost all of the time, he was our friendly lion. But he did have a shadow, that shadow burden brilliant people carry around with them, that ability to cut someone in half at a glance, and occasionally it would come to the surface.

Once he asked us if we thought life was like a play, like Shakespeare suggests. Then he said my name and stared at me. "Jim Ellefson, can you say *'That you are here—that life exists, and identity, that the powerful play goes on, and you will contribute a verse.'*"

"Yeah," I said. "Absolutely. That is, I think so."

Some class tittering.

I had no idea he was quoting Whitman, even though the quote was from a reading recently assigned. How could I have known? For my part, all I could do was read a little bit of *Leaves*, and then stomp around all night in the rhythm of it. I was one of those dogs and kids in Walt's entourage. I was along for the ride, and I had no idea where the ride was going. All I knew was that everything in the world was different, even my own footfalls over the sidewalks. My vision wasn't blurred, but crisp; everything had an edge, and some of it hurt. Everything had a voice, and I was out there trying to listen.

But Jack wasn't finished with me.

"Jim, do you like Walt?"

"Yes, sir. I like his work, too."

Titter. Titter.

Jack smiled a little shyly and looked out the window. My mother suffered from southern belle syndrome, and that influence had seeped into my personal lexicon. I'd get on my "sir" and "ma'am" train and just choo-choo off into no man's land. It stood out at the wrong times—like this one, when you were about to make an ass of yourself in a college classroom. Drum roll. I'm on the high dive, walking to the very edge of a three-hundred-foot spring board. I'm about to do a mile-high triple back gainer with a half-twist into a glass of water.

"And what is it exactly that you like about Walt?"

At this point, the class could clearly smell blood. The Great White Shark had already made initial contact, a good bump in the chest, and was circling around back to swallow whole the entire entrée. A lot of faces were breaking into smiles, looking back at me. And for my part, I never had the poise or skill to lie, or lean on the perceptions or opinions of the famous and revered. I didn't know what Lionel Trilling had said about Whitman, or who Lionel Trilling was, for that matter. This information wasn't for me to know. I was too busy throwing rocks at birds and what's worse, then—and now—I couldn't have cared less. I had absolutely no guile. We were talking about literature—love, hate, pain, regret, and death, and your true self has to come to the forefront, to the surface, and break a little sea ice on discovery. The real you comes to the surface, the only trouble is that sometimes the real you is a complete and utter idiot.

"I like the way he makes me feel," I finally said, and then went under the surf in the wash roar of class laughter, brine, and sand. Riptide. Rolled and pounded on the bottom of the ocean, where many women and men have salted the water with their own bones. In the roll and crunch, I was pulled out deep, salt filling lungs, kelp between my toes, pulling at my ankles, razor clams cutting right through the corneas of my eyes.

For his part, Jack stared at the floor and smiled and nodded for a few seconds, waiting for a little quiet. It was like that in the early 70's in a university classroom. Some professors were there to mock and ridicule poor suffering lame hick dopes like me on their way to an undergraduate degree. When you walked into the football stadium at graduation, you needed a mortarboard hat a couple of sizes larger to accommodate the four years of lumps on your head. I think mine must have been a size fifteen. Then, after you got your degree, you were free and justified to pass along that malevolence and bad will to someone else. House rules. Don't like it, get the hell out.

When Jack finally looked up, he didn't have a fin up on his back. Instead, he was wearing his lifeguard suit with a red cross on the chest. He laughed a little bit, but his eyes were watery. Baby blues.

"I like the way Walt makes me feel, too."

Jack also led us all to believe—via Walt—that we had the potential to become great. Jack would stick out his hand like he was offering us a peach.

"You have to understand that Walt was a joke, a hack editor-writer-poet living on Long Island. No one took him seriously—like us." Like us. That was part of Jack's message, too. Greatness was something available to all of us, something like a writers' American dream, definitely on the menu at the restaurant. Yes, I'll have the Mexican Combo platter, the side of guacamole, keep the Corona coming, and I'd like some greatness with that, please. Or maybe it was like the GI Bill Jack had gone to Columbia on. Once you slipped in the door past the academic bouncer, you just had to work to get it, and the more you worked, every once in a while, a gift would be delivered right into your trembling fingers. I'd get my poems back from Jack, and in the margins there were comments like: "This piece brought me to tears. Driving, sensational rhythm. Gem of a poem. Magnificent. This poem has arrived. Don't touch it." And I'd feel myself inflate, armor for skin, glide in my stride, pep in my step, pounding the empty, middle-of-nowhere Pennsylvania mountain collegiate streets at night looking for an angry literary fix, or feel the blood of the horse become my blood as we charged into Crimean cannon fodder.

About a year later while spending the evening playing music and drinking at a house party with my no-good band friends, I became engaged in drunken conversation with another English major writer type who said, "I was going to teach high school, but now I'm not so sure. Jack McManis has seen something in my work that he wants me to develop. He said my poems bring him to tears." I'd spend a few trips wondering about it all as I walked around campus. Maybe Jack just had a few things he said "to all the girls" or maybe he really did see talent in everybody, or maybe that pile of student papers on his desk got so immense that he lost a little traction with his comments and brought out a rubber stamp.

All of it would pass through my mind when I sat in Jack's office for the one-on-one sessions we did with my poems. I never did realize what an honor it was to be there—or how much of his personal time he was giving me. I just thought he had nothing else to do. He had a poster on the wall that read: "Happiness is for peasants: Give me ecstasy." And I suppose that's what I was getting. Jack would systematically fall into a trance over the poem, and then tell me everything he liked about it, everything that worked, everything that was original. Nod. Smile. Look out the window.

He often skipped what he didn't like, or said something like: "Not sure about line three" or "maybe something else." At the time, I grew impatient with the lack of specifics. I wanted someone to tear my work apart and tell me what to do, so it would rise to an entire new level. I wanted to join the poetic Marines at Iwo Jima, or go under Apache writers' training, literary boot camp. I wanted to be a literary Spartan at Thermopylae, live and die with Coleridge by writing poems with the "best words in the best order," consort with Dickinson and write poems that got physical—where I could feel as if the "top of my head were taken off." I wanted something more than "not sure."

Later, I'd see and experience it all in graduate school, where students got so confused and disoriented about their own aesthetics under the guise of tough love, that by the time they received their advanced degrees, they were creating ultra-pasteurized, homogenized milk. Jack's method was far more subtle. He got so under your skin that you'd never be able to get him out. He never told us what to do, how to do it, or where to go. He did, however, suggest that whatever we were doing, we should do some more of it.

"You could do so much more. Produce, produce, produce."

Produce.

"So what is it that you want to do with your work?" he'd ask me.

I had no answer.

One of the last times I visited Jack, he showed me a scrap of paper he had found in his desk when he first arrived at Penn State in 1957. Jack had replaced Theodore Roethke on the faculty and had inherited Roethke's uncleaned-out desk. It was mostly filled with the typical stuff—broken pens and paper clips—but apparently, stuffed back in a side drawer was a scrap of a poem: "His fingers and wrists were tattered and charred / an artist's life is terribly hard."

"Not a very good poem, is it?" Jack asked.

"No, I guess not," I said, trying to agree. "But he sure wrote some good ones, didn't he?"

Jack smiled, looked out the window and nodded, turned back to me and seemed to be waiting for some kind of response, but I never knew what to say. I knew Jack for five years; I took five of his classes. In some ways, I never really did go to Penn State as an undergrad. I went to Jack School—did an independent study with him, spent plenty of time in his office, he was my advisor. Still, I always felt uncomfortable. We weren't *friends*. I was always awkward. Uneasy. I felt like he was always slightly disappointed in me, like I could do "so much more." He was trying to show me something, and I was too dumb to follow the bread crumbs.

Over forty years later, I'm still following his trail. I wear running shoes just in case I have to set off some depth charges on the deck of a destroyer or if everybody's dancing in the aisles at the Apollo, I'll be ready to cut some rug. And I found a white tweed coat and a V-neck tennis sweater at the upscale resale store outside Middlebury College, and I go into my classes, first day, Jack-style, with my polo collar fin up, internally reciting: *"Half a league, half a league, Half a league onward, All in the valley of Death rode the six hundred"* in my devil-dog James Earl Jones. Maybe my lips move. I hope not, but I'm not sure, in the way all intense insomniacs are not sure of anything they do.

For every three days, I can say that I sleep a good five hours. And when I go into a classroom, I don't go in alone. I have an entire entourage with me: Li Po's kissing the moon and paying for it; Hart Crane is falling through space, just about to hit the water; and I have three books clutched to my chest. My smile has gotten shy, and I look at the floor when I speak; I look out the window, smile and nod, and I tell them everything I know with my two fried egg Walt eyes.

I tell them how, after two days of holiday drinking, I fell into two Christmas trees in one night, breaking one family's antique heirloom Dresden glass ornaments. I tell my students I could open up an apology store on Church Street in Burlington, Vermont called Jim's Redemption Center. At my desk, I wear my coat like a cape, and tell them Walt was some editorial hack living on Long Island when he had a spiritual experience. I tell them Walt's hair and beard turned white overnight. He could be seen walking the streets of Washington followed by an entourage of smiling kids, dogs, cops, grandmothers, the war wounded, the insane. Walt knew Lincoln and Lincoln knew Walt. And when my people write something fearless and beautiful, intensely original, I smile and nod, look out the window, and make sure they pack their words up in their old kit bags for the journey—which will be endless, by the way. The bread crumbs will go on forever.

That's right. I smile and nod and try to stand up straight, set my brawler shoulders back, chin up, bat my baby blues, weaving almost imperceptively in the under-tow of it, in the wash and roar of it, as the waves grind all of our bones into sand; I stand there, completely and utterly under the influence.

THE WAY IT WORKS

"...I am not afraid to leave you, yet I love you,
You express me better than I can express myself,
You shall be more to me than my poem."

Walt Whitman

I painted the old house like a schooner, chrome
green hull, bright white railings, a demonstrative
big red front door, and I painted that house so I could
take a rogue wave if I had to. She floated
over the snow half the year, got swallowed
into the hillside the rest.

> The soil was deep, humming
black, and by late June, the entire farm was a blooming
dog rose, air so thick you could climb
straight into the tree-tops. You could
ride around on that air, or disappear into some black
fold corner, the floor boards of that old house
vibrating your bones.

> On foggy mornings, chickadees
would hang upside-down from the brim of a baseball
hat, and if you woke before sun-up, the place smelled like sand
dollars and star fish. At night, entire patches of the woods' ground
glowed, and you could hear singing and drumming far
off in the hills.   A stream ran through the place full
of brookies
and rainbows, and there was an orchard, too: Evans
cherries, Staceyville pears. Black Oxford, Keepsake, Yellow
Transparent apples.

I meant to cut out the brush scraping
against the east side of the shop, replace the bird-shattered
windows, hook-up a wood stove, and move the heirloom
Concord grapes off the south wall, and I meant to dig-out
the orchard well, install a cast iron hand pump, pipe
water under the gravel road to the horse barn, and cut
an access into the cedar swamp. I meant to lay
an oak floor in the original summer kitchen, pull-up
the hatchway on the cow barn's north gable, and bull-doze
a pond somewhere between where the water seeps-out
of the east larch hillside and the cattail marsh.

                                    And I meant
to tell her how something in my chest had cooked up into dried
blood and busted bird bones. I meant to tell her how I had run
out of air. I couldn't lay down anymore in all that bottomless
dark water and sick bed.

                        My last trip out, I pulled off some
lupine seeds, dug up the horseradish and rhubarb, piled
my tools on a pile of sawn lumber, and drove out of those hills.

The old house was fitted together like a Northumberland
Schooner. There was fiddle music, snow-shoe hares, and wild
blueberry pie a la mode every night, and that brook
was full of rainbow trout.

                        Good-Bye Rose Island Farm.

SAVE THAT TIGER

"Reexamine all you have been told,
At school at church or in any book,
Dismiss whatever insults your own soul."

Walt Whitman

July fourth. Summer lake. Fish jumping. Fireworks. Four
old friends. A party boat floats by tromboning kitsch
jazz standards while four friends row all the way
into midnight. Four friends sit in green chairs. Four
friends laugh on a screen-in porch until
dawn, and then all four eat huge pancakes in the cool
humid morning. Amber maple syrup. Hot coffee. Four

old friends, and a year later, three friends. You see
one has tragically and unexpectedly died, and then
two, and before long, only one is left on the red
porch listening to the jazz boat motor by. There are
countless hours of remorse and rowing alone, tears, face
ceremoniously buried in hands—a real
full-blown lament. The last guy puts in a few

months of this until he gets mad, and when he gets
mad, he gets even. He goes to the local
hardware and antique variety and buys every
clock they have, and then systematically
rearranges all the numbers backwards. No
kidding. He rearranges the numbers so old
Father Time's got to do an about-face. And then
he winds all the clocks up, plugs them all in, sits

back in his green rocking chair with a little
self-satisfied grin on his face and waits. He only

has to wait a few months for the first friend to return
—and then two friends wait in green chairs for the third
—then three wait for the fourth, and then
before you know it, the team's back to full
strength—shouting and hooting in considerable
reverie. And as if they're all telepathically
connected, they simultaneously rise and smash
all the clocks. Yes. Into smithereens. Not one is
spared, and in an unrestrained rampage, all four send
dictatorial springs, gears and numbers to the ten

directions, never to assemble again. The friends
now converge on the lake every year, and after
midnight can be seen rowing their boat from misty
shore to shore, scaring up roosting herons and sleeping
catfish. Some vacation people say it's rather
depraved how the four have successfully defied the great
fundamental laws of nature, but the friends just
smile when confronted by such talk, tilt their snowy
heads together, ever intent upon putting their
inexhaustible energies into intricate—if not
amusing—renditions of the classic standard, "Save
That Tiger," proving once and for all that nobody
ever dies, that there are no phantom black
holes in our lives, and that any dedicated
quartet can hold a distinguished harmony forever.

RECONSTRUCTING THE ENTIRE INSTITUTION
AT BROWN'S STABLES

"They go! they go! I know that they go, but I know not where they go…"
Walt Whitman

She had a piece of inner tube flapping
over the pad lock on her barn door. Everything
else was put together with bale string, bent
over nails, feed bags—order: bushel baskets
full of worn-out horse shoes, good jelly
jars, dry stove wood
                              —huge bamboo feather rake
hanging next to a home-made shovel handle
twitch, sacred swallow nests, high top rubber
riding boots, antique hay chopper, ancient
fair posters tacked over the blustery
cracks in the wall
                              —a white enameled steel
veterinary cabinet floating around leaking
bottles of Absorbine, pine tar, Special
Green, Ivory Snow laundry detergent
next to the displayed Crosby
dressage saddle, Confederate army issued
hackamore, moth eaten stained
back pads
                              —a black dial wall phone with a forty
foot extension cord right under the hand-
painted yellow cardboard sign that read—in giant
crimson letters: RIDE AT YOUR OWN RISK.

In Dreams, Walt Forsees The Future

Some of the wounded and dead in the military hospital
were women. I didn't recognize anyone's
uniform, but every room was full, and gurneys
gridlocked the hallways. The entire building towered
into its own colossus by the sea, accessible by its own
shipping line, train, trollies, flying machines. Casualties
drained past the armed guards and through the doors. I asked
a rosy-faced soldier with a missing left leg
if I could write for him, a letter to his mother or father? "Do you
have a sweetheart?" I asked him. "Would you like a horehound
candy, rice pudding, play twenty question?"

                                                                   He kept

rocking, looking to the left of my face, mouthing
words. Two wires were coming out of his
ears and into a small black box he drummed with his thumbs.

I asked a child dressed up as a doctor, "Who are we
fighting? Are we still at war?"

                                                      The boy grinned and shook his
head—told me there was a fine restaurant on the basement
floor, today serving "awesome kale frittata." "You'll get
a senior discount," he said, patting my back, pointing
down the packed Claude Monet inspired hallway, where metal
doors opened and closed on their own.

                                                         Inside a talking

box at the café, the man running
for president was the same orange-haired
clown I had seen at Barnum and Bailey's spinning
plates, singing "God Bless America" in operatic baritone while

the crowd swooned and cried. His pants were sewn together
thousand dollar bills with the miniature portrait of Grover
Cleveland turned towards the light, and every
once in a while, he'd drop those pants to his ankles
for laughs.

And for the first time in our nation's history, no
one would have guessed, and surely it's about time, an animal
was running for the highest office. Yes, there was a she-
wolf dressed up in $12,000.00 Italianate grandmother's tweed
clothing. Evidentially, someone had taught her how to
speak, smile, and point both her right and left
paws at a camera.

And then there was a wind blown snowy-
haired old man with wings who spoke to chanting
thousands while wild birds landed on his lectern. "I believe
in this country, if we stand together, we can guarantee
health care to all people as a right, we
can provide decent paying jobs, we can
make public universities and colleges tuition-
free and make sure every
person in this country gets the education
they need and desire, we can
lead the world in transforming
our energy system and combating climate change, we can
demand that the wealthiest people in this country start paying
their fair share of taxes. And we can do this when
millions of people stand up, fight back, and create
a government that works for all of us. This is not some
Utopian dream: it can happen."

The orange clown dropped his Grover Clevelands, mugged

a sigh, and called him "crazy."

The she-wolf-woman bared
her teeth and snarled, "Oh, the better to eat you with."

Me, round shouldered and head down, I hit the hot black
road out of the city, and in the distance, I could see a beach
covered with red and blue starfish. When I got
closer, the echinoderms turned into drowned little
boys in red shirts and blue shorts, faces washed hard into
gravel and sand. When I held the children in my arms, they all
became alive again, thousands of them, a red shirt and blue
shorts sea of laughing boys and old man, arms linked, holding
hands, the cold foamy tide rolling around our ankles, each boy
shouting, "Come on, Uncle. Hurry. There's so little
time. Which way's America?" And I said, "Follow me."

Starry Union

See! see! see! where how the sun is beaming gleaming blazing!
See! See! see! all the bright stars, gleaming!
North, or South, or in order westward beaming,
Union all! O' its Union all!
O its all for each one, & each one for all!

Walt Whitman Bids Adieu To The Graduating Class Of The Bankrupt Backwoods Alternative College

What you really have to understand, ladies
and gentlemen, is that the problem comes
essentially down to the truth. Take
great literature for example. Sure
it's great, but does it fly the flag, or float
the boat for that matter? Or—OK—forget
the flag. Does it have real litmus
potential? For instance, my green and black

1966 Fairlane Ford was able to find
every banana peel on the Lord's great
highway, and you see, the same is true
of the study of great literature: it's
colorful; one gets stuck from time
to time; and it's classical in nature—
like that Ford. Well, I'm not talking about
Greece or Rome—but rather, let me
refer to the occasion where I stuck a deflated
football into the Fairlane's broken passenger's
side vent window to block unpleasant drafts—ten
below, ice cold beer, a little smooth music
bouncing off the olfactory reality of the pigskin. I
mean it was cold in that car. Truth. But I

suppose we were bound to come down to all the great
truths anyway: the truth in representation—like
in great art; the spoken truth—like when you
listen to me; and the truth in situation—as in

money. Or to be perfectly honest, let's put the truth
behind us, and let's talk about the way things

work—our thing, for example, this I talk you
listen thing we got going. So. Listen: No one
has anything to teach you, and what you must
know is that you are all perfect and beautiful
—so perfect and beautiful you will
rise to the top of any great body of dark
bottomless water as long as you always
remember. You must never forget. You will all
rise. You have my personal guarantee on this
matter, and just enough time left in your lives
to grow wings. So. All of you. Go. Now. You have
some work to do, and I'll be seeing you in my dreams.

Fomite

About Fomite

A fomite is a medium capable of transmitting infectious organisms from one individual to another.

"The activity of art is based on the capacity of people to be infected by the feelings of others." Tolstoy, *What Is Art?*

Writing a review on Amazon, Good Reads, Shelfari, Library Thing or other social media sites for readers will help the progress of independent publishing. To submit a review, go to the book page on any of the sites and follow the links for reviews. Books from independent presses rely on reader to reader communications.

For more information or to order any of our books, visit http://www.fomitepress.com/FOMITE/Our_Books.html

More Titles from Fomite...

Novels
Joshua Amses — *During This, Our Nadir*
Joshua Amses — *Raven or Crow*
Joshua Amses — *The Moment Before an Injury*
Jaysinh Birjepatel — *The Good Muslim of Jackson Heights*
Jaysinh Birjepatel — *Nothing Beside Remains*
David Brizer — *Victor Rand*
Paula Closson Buck — *Summer on the Cold War Planet*
Roger Coleman — *Skywreck Afternoons*
Marc Estrin — *Hyde*

Fomite

Fomite

L.E. Smith — *Travers' Inferno*

Bob Sommer — *A Great Fullness*

Tom Walker — *A Day in the Life*

Susan V. Weiss —*My God, What Have We Done?*

Peter M. Wheelwright — *As It Is On Earth*

Suzie Wizowaty — *The Return of Jason Green*

Poetry

Antonello Borra — *Alfabestiario*

Antonello Borra — *AlphaBetaBestiaro*

James Connolly — *Picking Up the Bodies*

Greg Delanty — *Loosestrife*

Mason Drukman — *Drawing on Life*

J. C. Ellefson — *Foreign Tales of Exemplum and Woe*

Anna Faktorovich — *Improvisational Arguments*

Barry Goldensohn — *Snake in the Spine, Wolf in the Heart*

Barry Goldensohn — *The Hundred Yard Dash Man*

Barry Goldensohn — *The Listener Aspires to the Condition of Music*

R. L. Green When — *You Remember Deir Yassin*

Kate Magill — *Roadworthy Creature, Roadworthy Craft*

Tony Magistrale — *Entanglements*

Sherry Olson — *Four-Way Stop*

Andreas Nolte — *Mascha: The Poems of Mascha Kaléko*

Janice Miller Potter — *Meanwell*

Joseph D. Reich — *Connecting the Dots to Shangrila*

Joseph D. Reich — *The Hole That Runs Through Utopia*

Joseph D. Reich — *The Housing Market*

Joseph D. Reich — *The Derivation of Cowboys and Indians*

Kennet Rosen and Richard Wilson — *Gomorrah*

Fomite

Stories

Fomite

Martin Ott — *Interrogations*

Jack Pulaski — *Love's Labours*

Charles Rafferty — *Saturday Night at Magellan's*

Kathryn Roberts — *Companion Plants*

Ron Savage — *What We Do For Love*

L.E. Smith — *Views Cost Extra*

Caitlin Hamilton Summie — *To Lay To Rest Our Ghosts*

Susan Thomas — *Among Angelic Orders*

Tom Walker — *Signed Confessions*

Silas Dent Zobal — *The Inconvenience of the Wings*

Odd Birds

Micheal Breiner — *the way none of this happened*

David Ross Gunn — *Cautionary Chronicles*

Gail Holst-Warhaft — *The Fall of Athens*

Roger Leboitz — *A Guide to the Western Slopes and the Outlying Area*

dug Nap— *Artsy Fartsy*

Delia Bell Robinson — *A Shirtwaist Story*

Peter Schumann — *Planet Kasper, Volumes One and Two*

Peter Schumann — *Bread & Sentences*

Peter Schumann — *Faust 3*

Peter Schumann — *We*

Plays

Stephen Goldberg — *Screwed and Other Plays*

Michele Markarian — *Unborn Children of America*